“I’m pregnant.

Caitlin breathed the words aloud, testing them on her tongue.

She was going to have Trey’s baby.

It still rankled that he hadn’t bothered to wake her and say goodbye in person. The note he’d left her said that he couldn’t stay in Seattle. His future as a rancher was incompatible with her life in the city, and he wouldn’t ask her to sacrifice her career. Still, making love with him had been deep and meaningful.

She’d never expected that they’d create a baby.

But now that they had, Caitlin couldn’t be sorry.

She just hoped Trey would feel the same way when she told him....

Dear Reader,

Welcome to Special Edition…where each month we publish six novels celebrating love and life, with a special romance blended in.

You'll revel in *Baby Love* by Victoria Pade, our touching THAT'S MY BABY! title and another installment in her ongoing A RANCHING FAMILY saga. In this emotional tale, a rugged rancher becomes an instant daddy—and solicits the help of Elk Creek's favorite nurse to give him lessons on bringing up baby.

And there's much more engaging romance on the way! Bestselling author Christine Rimmer continues her CONVENIENTLY YOURS miniseries with her thirtieth novel, about an enamored duo who masquerade as newlyweds—and brand-new parents—in *Married by Accident.* And you won't want to miss *Just the Three of Us,* Jennifer Mikels's tender love story about a high-society lady and a blue-collar bachelor who are passionately bound together for the sake of an adorable little boy. Then an estranged tycoon returns to the family fold and discovers unexpected love in *The Secret Millionaire* by Patricia Thayer—the first book in her WITH THESE RINGS series, which crosses into Silhouette Romance in September with *Her Surprise Family.*

Rounding off the month, Lois Faye Dyer will sweep you off your feet with a heartwarming reunion romance that results in a surprise pregnancy, in *The Only Cowboy for Caitlin.* And in *Child Most Wanted* by veteran author Carole Halston, a fiercely protective heroine hides her true identity to safeguard her nephew, but she never counted on losing her heart to the man who could claim her beloved boy as his own.

I hope you enjoy these books, and each and every novel to come!

Sincerely,

Karen Taylor Richman
Senior Editor

LOIS FAYE DYER

THE ONLY COWBOY FOR CAITLIN

Published by Silhouette Books
America's Publisher of Contemporary Romance

For my critique group:
Rose Marie, Bonnie, Cathy, Kate, Janine,
Colleen, Patty, Janice and Nora.
Everyone should have such good friends.

SILHOUETTE BOOKS

ISBN 0-373-24253-0

THE ONLY COWBOY FOR CAITLIN

This edition published by arrangement with Harlequin Books S.A.

Look us up on-line at: http://www.romance.net

Printed in U.S.A.

Books by Lois Faye Dyer

Silhouette Special Edition

Lonesome Cowboy #1038
He's Got His Daddy's Eyes #1129
The Cowboy Takes a Wife #1198
The Only Cowboy for Caitlin #1253

LOIS FAYE DYER

Winner of the 1989-1990 *Romantic Times Magazine* Reviewer's Choice Award for Best New Series Author, Lois Faye Dyer lives on Washington State's beautiful Puget Sound with her husband and their yellow Lab, Maggie Mae. She ended a career as a paralegal and superior court clerk to fulfill a lifelong dream to write. When she's not involved in writing, she enjoys long walks on the beach with her husband, watching musical and Western movies from the 1940s and 1950s and, most of all, indulging her passionate addiction to reading. This is her eleventh published novel.

Lois loves to hear from readers and can be reached c/o Paperbacks Plus, 1618 Bay Street, Port Orchard, WA 98366.

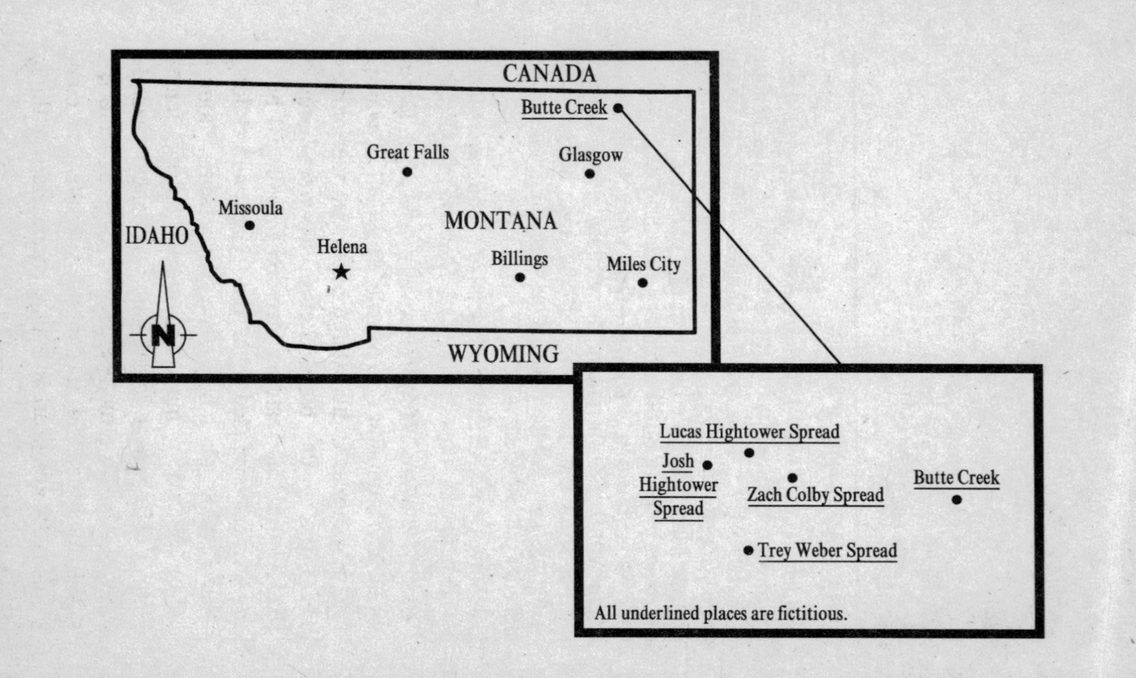
CANADA
Butte Creek
Great Falls
Glasgow
Missoula
MONTANA
IDAHO
Helena
Billings
Miles City
N
WYOMING
Lucas Hightower Spread
Josh
Hightower
Spread
Zach Colby Spread
Butte Creek
Trey Weber Spread
All underlined places are fictitious.

Prologue

Early September
Seattle, Washington

Trey Weber stood four feet away from Caitlin Drummond at the counter of a Seattle espresso bar, waiting for the waitress to fill a large paper cup with coffee. The brim of the black Stetson he wore threw a shadow over his features. Dressed in polished black cowboy boots, faded tight blue jeans and a long-sleeved white shirt beneath a black leather bomber jacket, he was a man who drew admiring female glances. His wheat blond hair was longer than the military cut she remembered, but his eyes were still brilliantly blue, and he still had a smile that could stop a woman's heart at twenty paces. He was thirty-six, and his youthful good looks had matured into lethal masculine beauty. His six-foot-four frame was broad-shouldered, slim-hipped and padded with heavy muscles. He was more devastating to her senses now than he'd been at twenty-six when he became her first lover.

My only lover.

And he'd broken her heart when he told her that the short two months they'd spent together were only a summer fling.

Trey Weber had left an imprint on her heart that had been impossible to erase or to replace with another man. After several dispassionate attempts, Caitlin had stopped trying, settling instead for a group of friends who accepted her refusal to date romantically.

I should have refused to help him search for the missing girl, Caitlin reflected. *I've managed to avoid him for nearly ten years and if I wasn't such a soft touch for kids in trouble, I would have told him to find his friend's runaway daughter himself.*

Trey reached into his jeans pocket, the faded denim stretching taut over a muscled thigh, and pulled out folded bills to pay for his coffee. Caitlin glanced quickly away from him, concentrating instead on shaking cinnamon and vanilla flavoring into her coffee.

''What do you think the chances are that we'll find her?''

His deep voice startled her. She looked up to find him standing within touching distance.

''I don't know,'' she confessed. She gestured at the silver-topped shakers. ''Sugar? Cinnamon?''

''No, thanks.'' He shook his head and leaned a forearm on the counter. ''If you don't know, then why did the police tell me that you're the best chance I've got of locating Jim's daughter?''

''Probably because I *am* your best chance,'' Caitlin answered coolly. She lifted the cup to her lips and sipped, watching him over the rim.

''But you haven't told me why,'' he prompted.

I shouldn't tell him. In all the years they'd been apart, he'd never contacted her. If he had, she thought, he would know the answer. *Tell him,* a small voice urged. *The sooner the two of you find the missing Amy, the sooner he'll go back to Montana and out of your life.*

''I wrote my doctoral thesis on the socio-economic reality of disenfranchised children—in short, street kids.'' She gestured toward the street outside the coffee shop. ''I've spent hours down here interviewing people. The kids grew to accept me. If they know anything about Amy, they're more likely to tell me than you or the police.''

He smiled, a brief curve of his lips that caught at her heart.

''So you've spent time in Seattle searching for information and I've spent time in the army hunting for people. Who would have guessed that we'd wind up in the same business?''

''Is that why your friend asked you to search for

his daughter when she ran away? Because you're experienced at finding people?''

He shrugged. ''Probably. Jim and I spent some time together in South America so he knew what I did before I left the military.''

''Ah, I see. You're right—who would have guessed that we'd ever have anything in common?'' Caitlin tossed her stirrer into the trash bin. ''Ready to go?'' She turned to him, bracing herself for the impact when her gaze met his. Even though she'd prepared herself, still her heart stuttered and caught before resuming a slightly faster regular beat.

''Sure,'' he answered, stepping aside to let her precede him from the narrow coffee shop.

Caitlin moved past him and out into the night. Rain fell in a steady downpour, blurring the outline of the old-fashioned street lamps that marked Pioneer Square. She paused under the shop's awning and opened her umbrella, suppressing a quick shudder as the damp chill of the late night air slipped beneath her raincoat.

''Where to now?'' Trey asked.

Caitlin pushed up her sleeve and peered at her watch in the dim light. ''It's almost midnight. Let's try the Rusty Nail.''

''A bar? Do they let kids in?''

''Not legally, but the owner isn't strict about how old his clients are as long as they have money. And the side alley is a gathering place for street kids. Six restaurants have back doors that open onto the alley, and the kids often find food there. I think it's worth trying. Even if Amy isn't there, there's a good chance that some of the kids I interviewed when I worked on the university study will be."

Trey shrugged and nodded. "This is your town. If you think it's worth a try, I'm willing."

"I think it's the best place to look," Caitlin confirmed. She gestured down the sidewalk. "It's three blocks this way."

Trey declined her silent offer to share the umbrella. The only concession he made to the rain was to hunch his shoulders against the steady drizzle that dampened his jacket and dripped from the brim of his Stetson.

Caitlin walked quickly, all too aware of the man who walked silently at her side. The sexual tension stretched taut as wire between them. It mattered not that they kept words at a minimum. Their bodies were carrying on the long conversations of want and need.

I have to handle this until we locate Amy, Caitlin lectured herself silently. *Then he'll go back to Montana, and I can try to get my life back to normal.*

Unfortunately, her heart and body were urging her to ignore her mind's practical advice.

She wanted him. Her heart ached, and she yearned to hold him, be held by him. Their brief, passionate affair when she was eighteen had left her unable to love anyone but him, and now that he was here, close enough to touch, it was difficult to remember that she'd been burned once by that fire and shouldn't chance the flames again. It didn't help to know that Trey wasn't immune to the heat that simmered between them, either. She was too aware of him to miss the telltale signs of interest.

Two hours later, soaked to the skin, Caitlin unlocked the door to her apartment and pushed it open before turning to look at Trey.

"Well, I guess this is goodbye," she said, unable to smile. "If the kids were right and Amy is at the youth shelter, you'll be on your way home tomorrow." Caitlin wanted to reach out to him, but instead her fingers clenched the plastic grip of her umbrella handle. She'd thought about this moment constantly since learning that Amy had been found, dreading the necessary pain of saying goodbye.

"I guess so."

His voice was deeper than normal, oddly husky. Caitlin wondered fleetingly if he'd caught a cold, for he was drenched, his clothing just as wet as her own.

She uncurled her fingers from around the umbrella and held out her hand. "I'm glad you found your friend's daughter. Have a safe flight home."

Trey's gaze dropped to her outstretched hand, and he went perfectly still, hesitating before he took her fingers in his. His lashes lifted, and his gaze searched hers. "After all the years we've known each other, can't we do better than a handshake?"

Caitlin didn't answer, couldn't answer. Riveted by the warm hand that enclosed hers and by his unreadable gaze, she couldn't summon her voice to say no. Instead, she watched helplessly, her heart beating frantically as he stepped closer and slowly lowered his head until his mouth found hers.

Caitlin forgot that they were both still dressed in layers of wet clothing. She forgot that the rain had drenched them both, forgot the chills that had chased goose bumps across her skin only moments before. The tentative, warm brush of lips against lips that began with such heart-wrenching sweetness blazed out of control with the swiftness of a match tossed into gasoline. Trey kissed her as if he were starving for her, fusing her mouth with his in a hot, open-mouthed, wet kiss that sent her straight from nervous anticipation to full-blown arousal in seconds.

Long moments later, he lifted his lips a fraction of an inch, his gaze searching hers for acquiescence before he slipped his arm around her waist and crowded her over the threshold into the apartment, kicking the door shut behind them. Caitlin barely had time to register the need that blazed in his eyes and to feel a surge of satisfaction that he was as out of control as she before he lowered his head and took her mouth again with unerring precision.

She wrapped her arms around him and held on.

The few short hours until dawn weren't nearly long enough to slake desire too long denied.

She never once thought about consequences.

Chapter One

"I can't be pregnant."

Caitlin Drummond threaded her fingers through her hair and swept it off her forehead, tucking a raven-black strand behind her ear. She glanced at the clock once more before pacing to the glass patio doors. It was after six p.m., but the sunlight still warmed the carpet beneath her toes. Outside, potted geraniums and hanging baskets of fuchsias bloomed in a glorious burst of pink and red blossoms, their glossy leaves a deep, luxuriant green in Seattle's late-September sunshine.

A small black and tan dachshund sat on his haunches and watched her pace, his ears lifting alertly each time she strode past him.

"Well, I can...it is possible, technically speaking,"

Caitlin muttered to herself, staring out the patio doors, seeing Trey Weber's face instead of the baskets of flowers. ''But it's not likely.''

The little dachshund barked, one short, sharp, inquiring yip.

Distracted, Caitlin glanced down and bent to swing him into her arms before she resumed pacing.

''We used protection two out of three times, Max,'' she told the little dog. ''So I'm probably not pregnant. I'm sure I'm just late. The stress of seeing Trey and telling him goodbye again has probably thrown me off schedule.''

Max stretched his muzzle toward her and swiped at her chin with his tongue, barely missing.

''Hey, stop that.'' Caitlin shifted the little dog in her arms before glancing once again at the wall clock. ''Time's up.'' She lowered the little dog to the floor and hurried into the bathroom, Max trotting at her heels.

Moments later, she stared in disbelief at the test strip, stunned shock struggling with a flood of delight.

''I'm pregnant.''

She breathed the words aloud, then repeated them, testing them on her tongue.

''Pregnant.''

Holding the test strip, she walked mechanically into the living room and sank onto the sofa.

I'm going to have Trey's baby.

She blinked, trying to focus on the sunlight that poured through the patio doors, heating her bare toes and warming her thighs and calves beneath the hem of her shorts.

Max barked, jumping up to plant his front paws against Caitlin's bare knees in a demand for attention.

Caitlin blinked, disoriented, as she glanced around the sunlit apartment.

Trey had stayed one night with her. He'd been gone when she awakened the next morning, having left only a note telling her goodbye. Amy was located at a center for runaways, and by that afternoon Trey and the repentant seventeen-year-old had left for Montana.

And Caitlin had been alone again in Seattle.

I knew he wouldn't stay, she told herself as she picked up Max and cuddled the little dog on her lap. *But I expected more consideration from him than to wake up alone with only a note left on the kitchen table.* She frowned. It still rankled that he hadn't bothered to wake her and say goodbye in person. His note told her that he couldn't stay in Seattle. His future as a rancher was incompatible with her life in the city, and he wouldn't ask her to sacrifice her career. Despite the depth of his feelings for her, he saw no future for them. Though the note was carefully worded, she still felt uncomfortably like a one-night stand, when for her, making love with him had been deep and meaningful.

I never expected that we'd create a baby.

But now that they had, Caitlin couldn't be sorry.

"So, Max, now what should I do?"

The little dog cocked his head, eyeing her with interest, and barked once in reply.

Caitlin patted Max absentmindedly. ''I love him, Maxie,'' she murmured. ''But I'm not at all sure how he'll react when he learns that he's going to be a father.''

In the last ten years she'd earned a doctorate in sociology at the University of Washington, and spent long hours working with Seattle street kids in conjunction with an outreach program. After dealing with damaged and abused children, she strongly suspected that Trey's fatherless childhood and the emotional rejection he'd suffered at the hands of his alcoholic mother had left him badly scarred.

Her suspicions only deepened her love for him.

Despite the fact that she wanted to smack him for leaving her that damned note, could she find a future with him for the sake of their child?

Caitlin smoothed her palm over the flat plane of her belly. A child grew within her, created by making love with the man who owned her heart—who had always owned her heart.

She had options, she reflected. She was well-established in her career, reasonably happy with her life in the city and confident of her ability to financially support and raise a child on her own. But her heart urged her to go home to Montana where she and her baby would be surrounded by loving family and friends. Her conscience and sense of fair play also told her that her baby was entitled to know its father and that she needed to explore every possibility of finding a way to give the little one two parents.

To do that, however, she would have to face Trey.

Much as she loved him, the thought that he might feel guilt and reluctantly offer to marry her was too horrid to contemplate. She wanted far more from him than a forced marriage.

"I want him to love me as much as I love him," she murmured. "But I'm not at all sure that he's able to love anyone."

The sunlight on the deck faded to dusk, and dusk gave way to full dark. Caitlin drank herbal tea and paced the floor, pondering her problem, considering and discarding options until she arrived at several inescapable conclusions. What she also desperately needed from Trey was a return to the deep friendship and shared trust she had known from him as a child. In retrospect, she realized that trust had disappeared from their relationship the day that passion arrived and Trey saw her as a woman he desired.

After much soul-searching and weighing of options, Caitlin picked up Max and headed for bed, content with her decision to return to Butte Creek, Montana. Trey was an unofficial adopted member of her extended family, and she knew that their paths would cross often. Before her pregnancy became visible, she would decide how to tell him and her family about the baby and decide on a plan for their future.

Brooding about Caitlin Drummond had become a pattern for Trey since returning from Seattle two weeks before. He'd spent most of his days working himself to exhaustion in an effort to fight the urge to board the first plane back to her. He would have given in to the need if he could have thought of any way to work out a long-distance relationship with Caitlin in Seattle and him in Montana. Unfortunately, he couldn't think of a single plan that didn't require one of them to give up their current life and move. He couldn't ask Caitlin to give up her career, and he'd already spent far too many years away from the land he loved.

Now he was home, and home he would stay.

But Caitlin wasn't home. At least, not here in Montana.

Seeing her in Seattle had been a bittersweet experience. On the one hand, she had become the well-educated, brilliant college professor he always knew she could be. On the other hand, he knew that she'd moved forever beyond his reach. The glossy sweep of her black hair, the expensive cut of her suit, the subtle quality of leather bag and shoes, the elegant emerald studs in her small ears that matched the clear green of her eyes—all carried an unmistakable message that he hadn't missed. Caitlin belonged in the city and in the halls of academia—not on a Montana ranch with him.

I should never have looked her up in Seattle, he acknowledged grimly. He knew damn good and well that he might have found the missing teenager without contacting Caitlin. The truth was, he'd welcomed an excuse to call her, and once he'd heard her voice, he'd had to see her. Once he saw her, he couldn't keep from touching. And once he touched her, he was lost. No other woman felt like Caitlin, tasted like her, moved like her. And no other woman made him feel that sense of rightness, of coming home, of finding the missing part of himself. She made him burn, but worst of all, she made him yearn and ache for things he knew he shouldn't want and could never have.

Ten years ago he'd chosen to let her go to live the life she'd dreamed of since she was a child, a life that he could never share. How many years would it take to convince his heart that it could never have her?

"Hell," he growled in disgust.

Sick of his own company and frustrated with attempts to repair a water pump that refused to work properly, Trey drove to the neighboring ranch in search of its owner, Josh Hightower. Josh's pickup was parked outside the empty corral, and Trey braked beside it, then slid from behind the steering wheel. He strode to the barn and pulled open the smaller door to the left of the long wooden slider to step inside. The big barn's interior was dim, and he blinked against the sudden switch from bright October sunlight to shadow. He knew the barn as well as his own, however, and didn't wait until his vision adjusted, but set off down the wide center aisle toward the tack room in the back.

He hadn't taken two steps before he ran into someone. Someone clearly female.

His hands automatically lifted to catch her waist as the woman stumbled against him, her hair brushing silkily against the bottom of his chin. Trey drew in a deep breath and froze in shock. He'd know that fragrance anywhere.

"Caitlin?" He tipped his head back to look down at the precise moment she lifted her face from his jacket to look up at him. He barely registered the astonishment in her expression before she pushed away from him and stepped back.

"Trey...hello."

"What are you doing here?" He was dumbfounded, trying to grasp that she was real and not a dream conjured up by his imagination. "How long have you been in Montana?"

"Since yesterday—and I'm visiting my aunt."

Slowly the shock began to subside. His eyes adjusted to the light, and Trey realized that she didn't look pleased to see him. He wasn't sure what she was feeling, but he was certain it wasn't the same stunned mixture of dismay and delight that filled him. "Visiting your aunt," he repeated slowly, his brain considering what that meant. "Haven't classes already started at the university? How did you get away?"

"I've taken a hiatus," she responded, her tone carefully neutral. "I won't be teaching classes during fall quarter."

Trey tried to ignore the leap of hope that warred with wariness. "So, are you staying with Sarah for the next three months?"

"No."

His hope plummeted to earth, but his sense of survival told him it was best that she wouldn't be staying.

"I'll spend time with Sarah, but I'll also be staying at my grandmother's house and with Aunt Molly."

''But you *will* be in Butte Creek for the next three months.'' Trey couldn't contain a slow smile of anticipation.

''Yes, I will.''

''That's great.'' She didn't return his smile, and he shifted, restraining the urge to reach for her by tucking his hands into the pockets of his unbuttoned denim jacket. Nevertheless, his good sense lost out to need. ''I'd like to see you while you're here.''

Caitlin shrugged, crossing her arms protectively across her midriff. ''You're practically a member of the family, Trey. I'm sure we'll see each other.''

''That's not what I meant.'' He wished she'd stop looking at him as if he was a casual stranger. ''Come to dinner with me tonight.''

Caitlin shook her head. ''No, Trey. I don't think that's a good idea.''

''Why not?'' He knew very well why it wasn't a good idea for him to spend time with her. It would only make it that much harder when she left. But he hadn't a clue why it wouldn't be good for her. Baffled, he stared at the stubborn set of her chin and knew he was in trouble.

''Because I refuse to carry on an affair with you in front of my family,'' she said bluntly.

Trey felt heat move up his throat and spread across his face. ''I only asked you to dinner,'' he growled. ''Not to a motel.'' But bed was exactly where he'd hoped they would end up, he admitted silently. It didn't help his frustrated hormones to know that she was right. Her family would worry about her and be disappointed in him if they found out he'd seduced their beloved Caitlin.

"Hmm." She sounded unconvinced. "Why don't you come to dinner here tonight? Lucas and Jennifer's family will be here, and Grandmother Patricia as well."

"All right."

"Fine."

She dropped her arms and moved forward, pointedly leaving space between them as she headed for the door behind him. Frustrated, Trey reached out and stopped her, his hand closing around her upper arm. She halted immediately.

"Let me go."

"Not until you tell me what I've done to make you treat me like something you just found stuck to the bottom of your shoe."

Her eyes lit with bright, angry sparks. "Your manners are atrocious," she said flatly.

Trey glanced at his hand that gripped her arm. "I'll let you go if you promise not to run away before you answer me."

She shook her head impatiently. "Not now—in Seattle."

Memories of Seattle, combined with the familiar smell of Caitlin's perfume and the feel of her arm under his hand, slammed into Trey. Touching her had been a mistake. Even through the layer of cloth separating his hand from her skin, the feel of her slim arm beneath his fingers roused a craving for more.

"What about Seattle?" His voice was husky, and a full octave lower than normal.

"I would expect a one-night stand to say goodbye in person, not leave a note."

Oh, hell. That damned note. He knew he should have talked to her, but he hadn't trusted his ability to be realistic if she'd asked him to stay. He knew himself too well to believe he could have refused her if she'd wanted him.

"I didn't want to wake you. You hadn't been asleep for more than an hour or two, and I had to be at the youth home by eight o'clock." That much was true. Trey didn't see any cause to tell her the other reasons he had for not waking her. It wouldn't solve anything, only create more problems between them.

Caitlin lifted a brow. "Oh, right."

"It's the truth, damn it." Suddenly her earlier statement registered, and he frowned, his fingers tightening. "And what the hell do you know about one-night stands?"

She didn't answer. Her silence was damning, and Trey jumped to a conclusion that set a match to his temper. He tugged her closer, and she stumbled, falling against his chest. He wrapped one arm around her waist and locked her hips against his, buried his other hand in the thick silk of her hair to hold her still and lowered his head, his mouth finding hers.

Weeks of pent-up frustration and suppressed desire poured from Trey into that kiss. He molded her slim curves to his while his other hand cradled the back of her head and his mouth relearned the shape and taste of hers.

He moved so swiftly that Caitlin barely had time to protest before she was swamped by her own need. Despite the bulk of their open jackets, she slipped her arms around his neck and pressed frantically against him, trying to get closer but frustrated by the layers of clothing. Trey groaned against her mouth. His hand left her hair to slip beneath her jacket and close gently over her breast. The warm, painfully arousing touch of his palm cupping her sensitive breast shocked her to awareness, and she murmured in protest, her hands flattening against his chest to push him away.

Breathing heavily, Trey let her go. She took a step back from him, her green eyes stormy with arousal and regret.

"I promised myself that I wouldn't do this. I will *not* sleep with you, Trey. What happened in Seattle was one thing, but I won't carry on an affair with you under my aunt and uncle's noses."

Trey drew a deep breath and held it in an effort to slow his pounding heart before he exhaled on a long sigh. "We're not kids anymore, Caitlin. What we do or don't do is our business, not your family's. Besides, I'm not sure either of us can stop what's between us."

"We'll see." She walked past him to the door and pulled it open, pausing in the bright stream of sunlight to look back. "You're still invited to have dinner with us tonight."

Trey nodded in acceptance. "I'll be there."

She stared at him for a moment, her expression solemn, before she stepped into the sunlight.

He followed her to the open doorway, leaning against the doorjamb as he watched her walk across the lot that separated the barn and corrals from the white picket fence enclosing the yard and house. She moved briskly up the porch steps and disappeared into the house. Trey sighed. The fierce pleasure in knowing that she would be near for three months warred with the knowledge that he would suffer equal measures of pain when she returned to Seattle.

And return she would. Trey was as certain that she would leave Montana as he was that he wouldn't ask her to stay. Because he was all wrong for her and he knew it. Caitlin wanted the whole package: love, home and a family. He couldn't give her any of those things. He'd closed himself off emotionally in order to survive his childhood, and somewhere along the way he'd lost that inner component that taught humans about love, about being a husband and a father. Whatever that magic something was, he didn't have it, didn't understand it, and couldn't find it. He'd long ago accepted his own inability. Caitlin Drummond deserved more from life than a man who couldn't make her happy because he didn't understand love. And he cared too much to watch her heart break if he tried. That was why he'd left her that damned note in Seattle instead of kissing her awake and making love to her like he'd wanted to. That was why he lied to her all those years ago when he told her that the few months they'd spent as lovers were only a way to pass the time while he waited for his wounds to heal before returning to active military duty.

He wanted Caitlin to be happy. He didn't expect the same for himself. The years had taught him that craving Caitlin was a never-ending ache that he managed to endure only with time and distance separating them.

He wasn't anybody's idea of husband material, never had been, never would be. But that didn't stop him from wanting her.

Now she wants me to keep my hands to myself while she's here. Just how the hell am I supposed to do that? Resigned to spending more sleepless nights alone, Trey sighed heavily and left the barn to resume his search for Josh at the nearby machine shop.

Caitlin changed her clothes three times before dinner, finally settling on a thin green sweater tucked into narrow-legged jeans. The silver buckle on the black leather belt that circled her waist matched the brushed silver earrings and narrow bangle bracelets on her wrist. She considered several simple rings before leaving all but one of her fingers bare.

I don't want Trey to think that I took pains to dress up for him.

She kept makeup to a minimum for the same reason and settled for brushing her hair until it gleamed, satiny and smooth, under the bright bathroom lights. After a last assessing glance, she left the bathroom and ran lightly downstairs to the kitchen.

Aunt Sarah, swathed in a huge apron, was bent over the open oven door, basting a pot roast.

''Caitee!'' A matching apron falling almost to her ankles, ten-year-old Samantha bounced up from the table and dashed across the room. ''Hi.''

''Hi, Samantha.'' Caitlin smoothed her palm over the child's silky blond hair and tugged gently on the end of the long braid. ''What are you doing?''

''Cutting up veggies for the salad—and peeling potatoes. Yuck.''

She wrinkled her pert nose in distaste, and rolled her blue eyes expressively.

Caitlin laughed and glanced at Sarah, who closed the oven door and turned to eye her daughter before sharing a wry smile with Caitlin.

''She's a lot like you,'' Sarah commented. ''She likes peeling potatoes just about as much as you do.''

''You hate to peel potatoes, too?'' Samantha interjected, eyeing Caitlin with interest.

''Oh, absolutely,'' Caitlin said with firm conviction. ''But somebody once told me that since I loved to eat mashed potatoes, I shouldn't complain so loudly about peeling them.''

''Hmm.'' Samantha shrugged her shoulders in defeat. ''Yeah, I guess that's true. Mom's mashed potatoes and gravy are just about my favorite things—except for strawberry cheesecake.''

''Then you better finish your chores, young lady, or there won't be any mashed potatoes at dinner.''

''All right, Mom.'' Samantha sighed gustily and returned to her seat at the table.

"Don't you look nice," Sarah said, appraising Caitlin's appearance. "I love those earrings—and only one per ear. Your grandmother will be very pleased."

Caitlin laughed and fingered one of the dangling hoops. "Grandmother Patricia never did approve of quadruple piercing my ears, and she told me so, long and loud. I guess it's fortunate that as I grew older, the number of earrings I wore steadily grew fewer."

"Mom says Grandmother Patricia is a member of the fashion police."

"Samantha!"

"Well, you did, Mom," the ten-year-old said with irrefutable honesty. "Grandmother Patricia doesn't like my favorite jeans—the ones with holes in the knees," she confided to Caitlin.

Caitlin pulled a paring knife from the holder atop the counter and took a seat next to Samantha. She picked up a potato and began to expertly remove the outer skin. "Well, kiddo, if it's any consolation, you're not the only one. She hated my favorite jeans, too."

"Yeah?" Samantha's eyes rounded with interest.

"Yeah," Caitlin confirmed. "But she's still my favorite grandmother."

"Yeah. Mine, too."

Caitlin and Samantha shared an affectionate glance before turning back to their chore.

Sarah pulled out a chair and joined them.

Caitlin eyed the mound of potatoes. "This looks

like enough food for an army. How many people will be here for dinner tonight?''

''Hmm, let's see.'' Sarah tossed a peeled potato into the pan. ''There's Jennifer, Lucas and their two kids. CeCe, Zach and their two. Annabel, Murphy, Charlie and your grandmother. Counting the four of us and you, Caitlin, that makes seventeen.''

''Oh, I forgot to tell you. Trey was here this afternoon and I invited him to dinner.'' Caitlin glanced up and met her aunt's gaze. ''That's all right, isn't it?''

''Of course,'' Sarah said comfortably. ''So we're an even eighteen. We'll seat the adults at the dining room table and put the children in here.''

''Oh, Mom,'' Samantha wailed. ''Does that mean that I have to sit with the little kids again?''

''It means that you'll eat your dinner in the kitchen with your younger cousins, yes.''

''I always get stuck with the little kids,'' Samantha grumbled, hacking away at the potato she held in her fist.

Sarah and Caitlin exchanged amused glances. Samantha was second youngest of the nine cousins, which irritated her no end.

The rumble of engines sounded, and Sarah rose to look out the kitchen window. ''Your aunt Jennifer and uncle Lucas are here, Samantha.''

''Is Alexie with them?''

''Yes.''

Samantha bounded up from the table, shedding her apron before racing from the room in a blur of flying blond braid and long legs.

"I swear," Sarah said with a sigh. "That child never walks, she always runs."

"You're just envious of all that energy," Caitlin teased, joining her aunt to look out the window. A blue pickup pulled behind Jennifer and Lucas, and two young men and a lanky teenage boy climbed out. "Oh, good, Stevie is here with Wayne and J.J."

A third truck parked near the first two, the driver pausing to speak to Wayne. Caitlin's heart caught, and she forgot to breathe. Trey's long legs and slow saunter were too distinctive to mistake for anyone else.

Chapter Two

"Trey's here," Sarah commented.

Caitlin flicked a sideways glance at her aunt. Sarah's blue gaze held a depth of understanding and invited confidences, but Caitlin glanced away, out the window, unwilling to discuss Trey. "Yes, so he is." She dropped the curtain and moved away from the counter. "I think I'll go say hello to everybody."

She left the kitchen, crossed the living room and pulled open the outer door just as the new arrivals reached it.

"Caitlin!" Jennifer Hightower stepped inside and wrapped her niece in a warm hug before standing back to smile with delight. "I'm so pleased you're here. And Sarah tells me we'll have you for three whole months. Is that true?"

"Yes." Caitlin returned Jennifer's smile with affection.

"How did you..." Jennifer's question went unfinished when her husband lifted her aside and swung Caitlin off her feet in a bear hug.

"Hey, kid." Lucas grinned at Caitlin as he set her on her feet. "Who let you across the state line? I haven't seen you in so long I thought you'd been banned from Montana."

Caitlin laughed and reached up to plant a warm kiss against his cheek. "You could have come to visit me in Seattle, you know. The road allows traffic to flow both ways."

"Nah." Lucas's eyes twinkled. "I knew you'd give in and come back to see me sooner or later."

Someone tugged on her arm, and Caitlin looked down into turquoise eyes the color of Lucas's beneath a curly mop of red-gold hair.

"Alexie." Caitlin bent to hug the eleven-year-old and was squeezed tightly in return. "How are you? My goodness, you're getting so grown-up. I'm not sure I would have recognized you if it weren't for your hair." She tugged gently on a silky curl and was rewarded with a beaming smile.

"Really?"

"Yes, really," Caitlin assured the girl solemnly.

"Wayne and Stevie keep telling me that I'm never going to grow up," Alexie confided.

"Oh, what do they know. They're just boys," Samantha offered, stepping past Alexie and into the living room. "Come help me finish my kitchen chores,

Alexie, then we can go up to my room. J.J. gave me a new bridle. It has hammered silver conchas on the head stall.''

Alexie's eyes rounded. ''Ooh. Okay.'' She glanced at Caitlin. ''I'm very glad you're visiting us, Caitlin.''

''Thank you, Alexie, so am I.'' Caitlin smiled at the shy little girl. Samantha caught Alexie's hand and tugged her toward the kitchen.

''Okay, I'm next.''

The drawled words drew Caitlin's gaze from the two girls.

''Wayne!''

Lucas's oldest son followed his father's example and caught Caitlin around the waist, swinging her in a circle.

Breathless, Caitlin laughed when he set her down. ''I thought Josh told me that you'd already left for college. I didn't think you'd be here tonight.''

''J.J. and I decided that we couldn't miss a family party, so we left campus after our noon class and drove straight through.''

''Don't let him fool you.'' Another male voice, colored with amusement, broke in. ''He really didn't want to miss Mom's cooking.''

Caitlin laughed and slipped out of Wayne's loose clasp. ''J.J., I've missed you. Give me a hug.''

The tall, blond-haired, green-eyed young man who held her close was a perfect foil for his cousin Wayne's dark good looks. J.J. was as close to a brother as Caitlin could get, and she adored him. He and Wayne had been only four years old and she twelve when she left her mother's home and came to live permanently with Sarah and Josh, J.J.'s parents.

"Hey, J.J., you're holding up the line."

Caitlin glanced over J.J.'s shoulder and found Steve Hightower, Wayne's fourteen-year-old brother. J.J. gave her a quick, bone-crushing last squeeze and passed her on to his cousin.

"So..." Steve grinned at her and awkwardly returned her hug and kiss. "What did you bring me from the big city?"

"Chocolates and espresso coffee beans," she answered promptly, laughing when his face lit with anticipation.

"Wayne can have the coffee, but I claim the chocolate. Lead me to it."

"I think Sarah took control of the box. You'll have to convince her that you really have to have some before dinner."

Steve headed for the kitchen, leaving Caitlin to face Trey in relative privacy. Last in line, he stood just inside the front door, watching her.

"Do I get a hug and kiss, too?"

His voice had the same deep, husky tone it held when they were making love, and Caitlin felt an immediate, powerful response. She glanced over her shoulder at the family members who stood or sat in the living room, chatting and laughing. No one was watching her and Trey, but still, Caitlin felt exposed.

"I, um, I don't think that would be wise—not here."

Trey's gaze left her and moved over the big room

before returning to brush her features again. "All right."

His tone held acceptance, and Caitlin drew a deep breath of relief. She wasn't good at denying how she felt when he touched her. She was immensely glad that he hadn't tested her in front of her family. She was feeling vulnerable and exposed, emotions she wasn't comfortable with, but she was beginning to think they might become the norm in the next few weeks and months.

"I, um, I think I'll go help Sarah finish dinner."

And before Trey could object, she was gone, disappearing through the door to the kitchen. He stared after her, wishing he could have tucked her under his arm and kept her close, knowing that it wouldn't have been enough.

Behind him, a loud knock rattled the door, and he dragged his thoughts from Caitlin and pulled the door open. Patricia Drummond, Caitlin's grandmother, and Patricia's friend Annabel Fitch whisked across the threshold and were greeted by a chorus of hellos. Trey was about to close the door when another car drove up.

"Hi, Trey," Zach Colby shouted. He and his wife, CeCe, exited the car with their two children, Jessica and Nick, who raced ahead of their parents and up the steps to the porch.

Once everyone was inside, the comfortable ranch house hummed with conversation and laughter. The four younger children adjourned upstairs while their older cousins discussed women and classes. Trey shared conversation and sipped bourbon with the men, listening intently for the sound of Caitlin's laughter from the kitchen.

At last dinner was ready. The adults took their places around the big dining room table, the children surrounding the long kitchen table. Trey was seated across the table and several people down from Caitlin. He passed platters, filled his plate and then emptied it, but if anyone had asked, he would have been hard-pressed to remember what he'd eaten or what it had tasted like.

Seated near Trey, Annabel leaned forward to speak to Caitlin. "It's so nice to have you home, Caitlin. I haven't heard why you decided to take this quarter away from your classes, though."

"I just decided that I needed a holiday," Caitlin answered calmly.

"It's about time," Josh said forcefully. "You were turning into a real workaholic."

"I was not," Caitlin protested, straightening in her chair.

"Oh, yes," Patricia agreed with a firm nod. "You were showing all the signs."

"Grandmother, that's not true."

"Well, you haven't been home for the last twelve months," Patricia pointed out. "And you used to take the summer months to visit us."

That was before Trey moved back to Butte Creek. Caitlin shot a quick glance down the table only to find Trey watching her with an unreadable gaze. She smiled faintly and returned her gaze to her grandmother.

"I don't think I remember Caitlin working less than full time since she went away to college," Lucas interjected before Caitlin could respond to Patricia. "I'd say the term 'workaholic' pretty much describes you. Not that I'm not glad you're here, but it's pretty unusual for you to take a long holiday."

"He's right," Josh agreed. "Are you sure there isn't something about this vacation of yours that you're not telling us?"

Caitlin swallowed a groan and managed a smile for her uncle. She loved her family, but they knew her far too well not to be suspicious. They were clearly hoping that she would satisfy their curiosity, but she didn't plan to tell them the truth for several weeks, perhaps longer. She needed to talk with Trey first, and she still wasn't certain how she was going to approach him with her news. "Gee, Uncle Josh, I wish I had something exciting to tell you, but the truth is, I've been teaching nonstop and decided to take a little time off. That's all."

"Hmm," Josh narrowed his eyes at her.

Caitlin smiled with what she hoped was convincing innocence. *That's my story, and I'm stickin' to it.* She disliked deceiving her family, but she saw no alternative. If they knew the truth, her future would be a nonstop topic of conversation, and Trey would be pressured unmercifully to do right by her. She really, really didn't want that to happen. She wasn't sure her uncle Josh was buying her story, however, and one quick sideways glance at her aunt Sarah found her exchanging looks with CeCe and Jennifer. *Even if the men accept my story, I doubt the women believe me. Oh, well,* she thought philosophically. *Until I tell them differently, they have no reason to suspect I'm hiding something.*

She casually peered down the table until she met Trey's gaze. It didn't reassure her to find a thoughtful expression in his blue eyes.

She definitely didn't want Trey speculating about hidden reasons she was home. Fortunately, Samantha chose that moment to pop her head around the corner from the kitchen.

"We finished dinner, Mom. Can we have dessert now?"

"I don't see why not," Sarah responded. She glanced around the table. "Maybe we're all ready for cheesecake?"

A chorus of confirmations answered her, chairs were pushed back, plates carried to the kitchen. Caitlin breathed a sigh of relief at the diversion and joined the rest of the family.

Later in the evening, after the dishes were washed and put away, everyone gathered in the living room.

"Daddy, can we go see the new horse?" Samantha asked.

Josh pulled his daughter on his knee. "Honey, I ate so much dinner, I'm not sure I can get up out of this chair, let alone hike all the way out to the barn."

"Yes, you can."

Josh groaned and glanced at J.J. ''Why don't you get your brother to go with you?''

''Nope.'' J.J. patted his flat midriff and grinned at his dad. ''Not me. I can't get up, either.''

''Don't look at me.'' Wayne shook his head. ''I should have stopped at one piece of cheesecake instead of two.''

''What a bunch of lightweights,'' Caitlin teased. Seated in a wing chair next to the sofa that held the sprawled figures of Wayne, Steve and J.J., she was lazily content. Max lay curled on her lap, and he lifted his head at her voice. ''Maxie and I will go with you, Samantha.''

''Me, too.'' Samantha's brother, twelve-year-old Justin, unfolded his long legs and pushed upright from his seat at Caitlin's feet. The yellow Labrador retriever lying beside him rose also, gazing expectantly at the boy, her tail wagging hopefully. ''You, too, Goldie.''

Samantha slipped off her father's lap. ''Come on, Alexie.''

''Put your jacket on, Samantha,'' Sarah said. ''I know we don't have snow on the ground yet, but the night air is too chilly to go out without a coat.''

''Okay, Mom.''

''We're coming, too.'' Zach and CeCe's nine-year-old son, Nick, and their daughter, twelve-year-old Jessica, abandoned their jigsaw puzzle and hurried to join Alexie and Samantha at the coatrack.

''Walking off dinner sounds like a good idea,'' Trey commented. He joined the five youngsters at the coatrack, shrugged into his jacket and turned to look inquiringly at Caitlin. "Are you coming?"

Caitlin glanced at the members of her family settled comfortably in the chairs and sofas in the big room. "Is anyone else joining us?"

The rest of the group shook their heads, declining the invitation. Reluctant though Caitlin was to leave the house with Trey, she couldn't deny the protective power of five preteens.

She set Max on the floor and rose to find her jacket.

No sooner had Trey pulled the door shut behind them, than the children clattered down the porch steps.

"Race you to the barn!"

The kids reacted to Nick's challenge with shouts, laughter, pounding feet and flying coattails. Maxie raced with them, his short legs a blur of movement as he tried valiantly to match Goldie's speed and longer stride.

Caitlin was left alone with Trey. She tucked her hands into her pockets and looked at him as they descended the shallow porch steps.

"Sarah told me that Charlie and Murphy have decided to retire and that you've leased their pasture south of the Hightower fence line."

"That's right." Trey paused to latch the yard gate behind them before they set off toward the barn. High above, the tiny sliver of moon gave faint light, throwing the wide barn lot into shadowy darkness. The October night was cold, with a brisk wind blowing off the buttes to the north of the ranch buildings, carrying the scent of sagebrush.

"Are you going to run cattle or horses?" she asked, genuinely curious about his plans.

"Both. But I hope to concentrate on raising quarter horses like Josh has done."

Light spilled out of the open barn doorway. Caitlin stepped inside, the warmth and familiar smells of hay and animals welcoming her.

The kids were halfway down the long corridor, peering through the rails of a roomy box stall. Caitlin reached them and closed her hands over the rails, leaning against their support as she stared with delight at the mare inside the stall.

"Oh, my," she breathed in appreciation. "She's a beauty."

Trey stopped behind her, so close that his chest nearly touched her shoulders. He braced one arm against the rails, his hand only inches from hers, his body sheltering her smaller frame.

"She is, isn't she? You won't find better bloodlines anywhere."

"Is Josh going to breed her with Zach's new stallion?"

"That's his plan. I can't wait to see the foal."

Voices hushed, the group murmured softly, discussing the mare's glossy coat and long legs. Before long, however, Samantha grew restive and suggested that they return to the house to watch a new video. Her cousins agreed, and before Caitlin could voice a protest, the kids and dogs disappeared out the door.

"I suppose we should go in," she began, turning from the stall. But before she could follow the children, Trey moved quickly, bracketing her against the rails with his arms.

"Not yet," he murmured, scanning her face. She returned his gaze warily, and he shook his head. "Caitlin, Caitlin. Why are you so afraid to be alone with me?"

"I'm not afraid to be alone with you," she said hurriedly.

"You've been avoiding me all evening. If you're not afraid of me, what's the problem?"

"There isn't a problem," Caitlin insisted. "You're imagining things. I haven't been avoiding you. It's just that I haven't seen my family in far too long, and we have a lot to catch up on."

"Hmm." Trey wasn't convinced, but he had other questions he wanted answers to that were just as important. "You never really answered Annabel and Josh's question at dinner. What convinced you to take a three-month break from the university—and I want the truth."

"I told Josh the truth. I needed a vacation, and it's been far too long since I spent time with my family." *And that is the truth,* Caitlin thought. *It's just not* all *of the truth—not quite. But I don't want Trey to know about the baby. Not yet.*

Trey searched her face, his stare intense.

"You're sure there's nothing wrong?"

"What could be wrong?"

"You're not sick?"

"Goodness, no." Startled, Caitlin spread her arms wide. "Do I look sick?"

His gaze moved over her, head to toe, then back up again. Caitlin felt the impact of his blue stare as surely as if he'd slowly run his hands down her body and up.

"No," he said, his voice slow and thick as molasses. "No, you don't look sick." He smoothed his fingertips over her cheek. "In fact, you look good enough to eat."

Caitlin closed her eyes against his seductive voice and the powerful lure of his work-roughened fingers moving gently against her flushed skin.

"Caitlin..."

His voice was deeper, rough with emotion.

Caitlin forced her eyes open and looked at him. His eyes were half-closed, their brilliant blue hot with need, his gaze fastened intently on her mouth. She stilled his fingers with hers, trapping them against her cheek.

"Trey," she whispered. "Please...let's go back to the house."

He wanted to say no. She saw the instant leap of refusal in his eyes before it was replaced with reluctant acceptance.

"If we have to. Are you sure you want to?"

"I'm sure we should," she countered.

The silence beat thickly between them, pulsing with raw desire. Then Trey drew in a deep breath, his fingers slipping from beneath hers.

"All right." He stared at her for one long moment.

"There's something you should know, Caitlin. When a woman runs, a man's natural inclination is to chase her. There's already enough heat between us to start a forest fire. You keep running away from me and you're liable to start something neither of us can control."

Caitlin stared at him, her pulse pounding. "You make it sound so primitive."

"Primitive?" His eyes narrowed, a muscle flexing in his jaw. "I guess that pretty much describes the way I feel around you."

The air hummed with tension. Caitlin was afraid to move for fear of triggering an explosion of the seething passion that pulsed between them.

"Trey, I..." Her throat closed, and she drew a deep breath before she could continue. "I want us to find a way back to being the friends we were before we became lovers. I don't want to lose you—you're part of my family."

"You want me to be your friend?" he asked bleakly, disbelief coloring his words. "That's all?"

"Not necessarily all. But I do want us to be friends—the way we used to be before the summer we made love."

Trey shook his head, his lips tightening in rejection. "I don't look at you and see a little girl anymore. We can't go back to the way it was, Caitlin."

"Then I don't know how to go forward, Trey." Tears welled, but Caitlin ignored them. How could she make him understand that she needed more from him than the incredible physical pleasure they found with each other? Especially when they had a baby on the way.

Trey's heart lurched. He'd never been able to ignore Caitlin's tears. He sighed and cradled her face in his hands, his thumbs gently smoothing the dampness from her silky skin.

"Oh, hell," he said with resignation. "Come here." He slipped his arms around her and tugged her forward, wrapping her close. She came willingly, fitting against him with a rightness that tore at his heart. He smoothed his palm over the sleek cap of her hair, sifting his fingers through the silky strands. "I don't want you to avoid me, Caitlin. You'll be here for three months. If we can't be lovers, at least don't walk out of rooms to keep from talking to me."

Caitlin's heart lurched. She'd never meant to avoid him. Spending time with him was an important part of her effort to discover whether she could have a future with him and their child. "I'm so sorry, Trey." She was immeasurably comforted by the haven of his arms, the solid strength of his body and the soothing stroke of his fingers in her hair. "I didn't mean to run from you. But I'm a little unsure exactly what our relationship is at the moment. Ten years ago I thought we had a future together, then you told me that I was nothing more than a pleasant way to while away a couple of months while you were recuperating. You left and I didn't hear a word from you until you asked for my help in Seattle a few weeks ago. You spent the night in my bed and disappeared before I woke up the next morning. I think it's pretty clear that I keep letting you into my bed and you keep leaving me and I don't think it's unreasonable that I don't want to go down that road again. Do you?"

"No. No, I don't think you're being unreasonable." He couldn't fault her logic. Nor could he tell her that he'd known he shouldn't have touched her. But sometimes his need for her grew too powerful for him to ignore. He should have been stronger. He should have left her alone, free of him. "But don't ever think that I left you easily."

The regret in his voice soothed Caitlin's bruised heart.

"I don't want my family to know that we're sleeping together, but when you kiss me, I tend to lose sight of all my good intentions."

Trey's fingers stilled briefly before resuming the gentle movements in her hair. "Then we have the same problem."

"And there's no solution," Caitlin said, bereft. "If neither of us can say no, we'll wind up in bed together."

Trey's mouth quirked in a wry smile. "And tell me again why that's a bad idea?"

"Because my uncles and cousins would come looking for you with a shotgun, and neither of us wants that."

"Mm." Trey wasn't so sure he would mind, but the repercussions would be impossible for Caitlin. "All right." He sighed, then released her, his hands sliding down her arms to settle at his sides. "Let's go inside."

* * *

Later that night, Trey stared out his bedroom window at the moonlit sky, his hands stacked beneath his head, the sheet and light blanket shoved to his waist.

Caitlin was hiding something. Despite her denials, his gut instinct told him that a deeper reason beyond vacation had brought her back to Butte Creek. There were secrets hidden behind her green eyes.

He shifted restlessly. He knew all about secrets. He had too many of his own, and too many of them were tied to Caitlin. He'd never meant to spend so many years in the military. His original plan had been to enlist and serve only long enough to earn college tuition. But after he'd purposely lied to Caitlin, telling her that their affair meant nothing more than a way to pass the time while he recuperated from being wounded in Colombia, he'd drifted. After sending Caitlin away to pursue her dreams without him, nothing in his life seemed to matter. And when the government offered him an obscene amount of money to reenlist, he'd signed the papers and flown to his new assignment.

The only good thing about those years in the military, he thought somberly, *was that saving those reenlistment payments created a bank account big enough to buy this ranch.*

The moon dropped toward the horizon. In the east, a band of pale gold presaged the coming of dawn, and outside Trey's window birds woke and set up a chorus of chirping.

''Hell,'' he growled in disgust, then threw back the covers and stalked naked to the dresser. He yanked open a drawer and found jockey shorts and socks, then slammed the drawer shut with a bang.

''Woof?'' The big dog sleeping on the throw rug in the corner lifted his head from his paws and fixed his weary gaze on Trey.

''Sorry, Chukka.'' Trey pulled on shorts and jeans and sat on the edge of the bed to tug on his socks and pull on boots. ''Go back to sleep.''

The black lab dropped his muzzle to rest on his outstretched paws, his sleepy gaze following Trey's movements as Trey shrugged into a long-sleeved cotton shirt. The dog gave a long suffering sigh and lumbered to his feet to pad after Trey when he left the bedroom and strode down the hall to the kitchen.

Trey switched on the coffeemaker and leaned against the counter waiting for coffee to brew while he brooded about Caitlin.

She wants us to be friends, so I'll try my damnedest to keep this platonic, he decided grimly. *And before she goes back to Seattle, I'm going to find out what's bothering her and fix it. If I can.*

Two days after her welcome-home gathering, Caitlin woke up feeling ill. Worse than ill. She felt terrible. She barely made it from her bedroom to the bathroom across the hall before nausea overtook her.

''Caitlin? Are you all right?''

Caitlin groaned softly, turned her cheek and opened her eyes. Sarah's jean-clad knees were at eye level. Before Caitlin could reply to her aunt's worried question, another wave of dizziness and nausea washed over her, and she was violently sick once more.

''Oh, sweetie,'' Sarah murmured, smoothing Caitlin's hair from her face.

The nausea passed, leaving exhaustion in its wake. Sarah smoothed a damp washcloth over Caitlin's face.

''Feeling better?''

Caitlin nodded mutely, eyes closed.

''Do you think you can make it back to your bed now?''

''Yes.'' Her response was shaky, and Caitlin was immeasurably grateful for Sarah's assistance from the bathroom to the bedroom.

Sarah tossed back the covers and tucked Caitlin beneath them.

''When did you start feeling sick, Caitlin?''

''Just this morning.''

''When you woke up?''

Caitlin nodded, her stomach rolling.

Sarah laid a palm on Caitlin's brow, frowning in confusion. ''You don't seem to be running a fever. Did you feel ill before you went to bed last night?''

''No,'' Caitlin whispered, one hand going to the blanket that covered her midriff.

''Don't get up, honey, just lie there. I'm going to get some soda crackers from the kitchen. I'll be right back.''

Caitlin nodded without opening her eyes, hoping that if she lay perfectly still, her head would stop spinning and her stomach would behave. She concentrated on breathing in and out, counting silently in slow rhythm.

Moments later, she heard Sarah enter the room, followed by the crackle of paper. She slowly opened her eyes and looked up. Sarah's gaze met hers with sympathy, and she held out a cracker.

"Here, Caitlin. Nibble on it. It will help settle your stomach."

Unconvinced, Caitlin eyed the innocent square cracker. "Are you sure?" she asked dubiously, one hand resting on her churning stomach.

"Positive." Sarah tucked the cracker into Caitlin's hand and watched while she lifted it to her mouth and took a small bite. "Women have been nibbling soda crackers and sipping tea to cure morning sickness for years."

Caitlin froze, her mouth full of cracker, and her stricken gaze flew to meet her aunt's. She squeezed her eyes shut at the perceptiveness she read there and turned her face away, groaning, her flushed cheek hot against the coolness of the pillow.

"Caitlin," Sarah said softly. She perched on the edge of the bed and smoothed the tangle of hair from Caitlin's forehead. "Why didn't you tell me?"

"I was going to," she mumbled, finally managing to swallow the cracker with a throat as dry as dust. "Just not yet."

"How far along are you?"

"About six weeks."

"Six weeks," Sarah repeated thoughtfully. "Early September. If I remember right, that was about the time that Trey went to Seattle to locate a friend's runaway daughter.''

Caitlin didn't answer.

''And ever since he returned, he's been as moody as a bear rousted from hibernation. Now I know why.''

Caitlin still didn't answer. Sarah sighed and stood.

''Go back to sleep, sweetie. With any luck at all, you'll feel much better when you wake up, and we can talk about this then.'' She bent and brushed a kiss against Caitlin's forehead. ''Try not to worry, Caitlin. You're home now. This will all work out.'' She started to leave, then added, ''I'm leaving the package of crackers on the nightstand. It might help if you could manage to get two or three of them into your stomach.''

''Aunt Sarah...''

Sarah paused, one hand on the door. ''Yes, Caitlin?''

''Thanks.''

It was mid-morning before Caitlin woke. She gingerly tested her stomach's stability by slowly sitting up in bed and was relieved to find that the earlier queasiness seemed to have passed. She showered, dressed and donned makeup before she headed to the kitchen.

''Hi.'' Sarah glanced over her shoulder and smiled at Caitlin. She picked up the steaming teakettle and poured boiling water into a rose-patterned china teapot. ''I heard the shower running and put the kettle on. Are you ready for real food, or just tea and toast?''

The thought of her customary breakfast of boiled egg and grapefruit made Caitlin's stomach roll. She shuddered and smoothed a hand over her midriff. ''Just tea and toast will be fine.'' Caitlin crossed to the counter and placed a slice of bread in the toaster, pausing with her finger on the lever. ''Do you want toast, Aunt Sarah?''

''No, thanks. I had breakfast with Josh hours ago.''

Caitlin glanced at the clock on the oven and groaned. ''I slept half of the morning away.'' She pushed the lever down on the toaster and leaned against the counter, arms crossed.

Sarah scanned Caitlin's face. ''I think you needed the rest. You look much better than you did a couple of hours ago.''

''I certainly feel a lot better,'' Caitlin commented. Behind her, the toaster pinged and the toast popped up. She pulled open the cupboard to collect a plate for her toast, found a knife, the butter and jam, and carried them to the table to join Sarah.

''Tomorrow morning I'll bring your tea and crackers upstairs. Don't even lift your head off the pillow until I get there,'' Sarah said firmly as she poured tea into Caitlin's cup.

''Yes, ma'am.''

''Oops.'' Sarah glanced at Caitlin and smiled wryly. ''Sorry—I forgot to say please, didn't I? It's just that I remember so well how awful I felt those weeks that I had morning sickness, and the only thing that really helped was when Josh brought me crackers—and tea—before I got out of bed in the morning.''

Caitlin grimaced at the memory of the overwhelming nausea that had hit her the moment she had lifted her head. ''Believe me, I'm willing to try anything that makes this go away. How long does it last?''

''It depends. For some women, only a few weeks. For others, the entire nine months.''

''Oh, no.'' Caitlin groaned and chewed another bite of toast, morosely contemplating the possibility of spending the rest of her pregnancy fighting nausea.

''But it's all worth it when you hold your baby in your arms.''

Caitlin brightened. ''I'm sure it is. I remember when Justin and Samantha were born, and I've never forgotten how you and Uncle Josh adored the new baby.'' She leaned back in her chair and glanced at her flat tummy. ''It's a little difficult to believe I'm pregnant since I can't see any changes, except for the morning sickness.''

''It's early days yet.''

''Yes, it is.'' Caitlin brushed toast crumbs from her fingertips and cradled her teacup in her hands, eyeing her aunt. ''All right. I'm ready, and I know you have a dozen questions.''

Sarah laughed. ''That's my Caitlin. You always face things head-on.''

Caitlin shrugged. ''In this instance, there's no use in pretending. You would have found out sooner or later. I never meant to keep my pregnancy a secret from you forever, Aunt Sarah. I would have told you.''

''I know you would have, Caitlin. Have you told Trey?''

Caitlin's fingers tightened over the fragile china cup. ''No, not yet.''

''Why not? Surely you're not worried that he wouldn't do the right thing?''

''The right thing?'' Caitlin frowned. ''Actually, I'm worried that he will 'do the right thing'—that he'll offer to marry me when I know very well that he doesn't want to.''

''Doesn't want to? Why would you think that?''

''Why would I think that?'' Caitlin's eyes widened in surprise. ''Aunt Sarah, why on earth would I think that Trey *wants* to marry me?''

Sarah's hands fluttered. ''My goodness, Caitlin, Trey Weber has been crazy about you since you were in high school! I'm only surprised that the two of you haven't gotten together before this.''

''Trey's never mentioned marriage, Aunt Sarah,'' Caitlin said. ''And I have no reason to believe that he ever seriously considered marrying me.''

''But he loves you, Caitlin. He always has.''

Caitlin's lips curved in a sad smile.

''Does he? I thought so once. We were inseparable the summer after I graduated from high school and he was home recuperating after being injured in Colombia. I was so sure that we'd be together forever, but he left me and flew off to his next assignment after making it perfectly clear that what we shared was nothing more for him than a summer fling.

''When he did finally come to Seattle, he didn't come to see *me*. If the police hadn't told him that his best chance of finding the missing girl was to contact me, Trey would have left Seattle without even telephoning me.''

''Oh, Caitlin,'' Sarah protested. ''I'm sure he would have made a point of seeing you. You were childhood friends.''

''No, Sarah,'' Caitlin said with faint bitterness and residual hurt. ''He wouldn't have.''

''But you don't know that for sure. I can't believe—''

''I do know.'' Caitlin interrupted her. ''He told me that he had no plans to see me.''

''Oh.'' Sarah's gaze filled with compassion and sympathy. ''Well,'' she said thoughtfully. ''I can understand why you need more than a shotgun wedding before you'll be convinced that marriage is what Trey really wants.''

''Yes.'' Caitlin nodded. ''Although, to be honest, I'm not sure what would convince me that he genuinely wants me.''

''Oh, I think the fact that you're pregnant pretty much confirms that the man wants you,'' Sarah said, a twinkle in her eye.

''Wanting to sleep with me is not the same as wanting to spend his life with me,'' Caitlin said firmly. ''I'm not willing to settle for a marriage that's less than what you have with Josh. I'm not an eighteen-year-old girl anymore with stars in her eyes. I need a real commitment from Trey. If he's not capable of that, then I'll raise my child alone.''

''When do you plan to tell Trey you're pregnant?''

Before Caitlin could respond, a noise on the utility porch captured her attention.

Her gaze flew to the open door and clashed with Trey's.

There wasn't a doubt in her mind that he'd heard. The stunned shock on his handsome face was proof enough.

How many times had she watched him come to their house over the years? Memories swamped her, a rush of longing shaking her. But she knew this wasn't the Trey who had teased her when she was twelve and he a young man of twenty. He was older, harder, a man whose emotional walls had only grown thicker, higher, more impenetrable with the life he'd lived in the years between.

She hadn't been able to breach those walls and hold him when she was eighteen. What ever had made her think that this time would be different?

Chapter Three

"You're pregnant?" Trey took two steps into the kitchen and stopped dead to stare at her.

"Yes."

"We're going to have a baby?" Delight poured through him. "I'm going to be a father?"

"Yes." Relief that he hadn't asked her if the baby was his seized her, her throat tight with emotion.

Josh moved into the doorway behind Trey, and Caitlin's gaze flew to his face.

"Uncle Josh." She breathed the words, unaware that her agonizing worry over what her beloved uncle would think of her impending motherhood was carried in her whisper.

The stern lines of Josh's face softened, concern warming the vivid blue of his eyes. "Caitlin, why didn't you tell us days ago?"

Caitlin was aware that Trey stiffened, but she kept her gaze fastened on Josh. ''I wanted to talk to Trey first. I didn't want to mislead you and Sarah, but I needed time to sort things out.''

''There's nothing to sort out.'' Trey's deep voice was grimly resolute. ''We'll get married.''

Caitlin sighed. ''No, Trey.''

''No? What do you mean, no? You're pregnant. Of course we're getting married.''

''Not necessarily,'' she said evenly. ''Not unless we're sure it's the best thing for the baby.''

''How could it not be best for the baby to have his parents married to each other?'' Trey was so taken aback by her refusal he could barely comprehend that she truly meant what she said.

''It wouldn't be best for my child to live with parents who were forced to marry when they didn't really want to.'' Caitlin's voice was calm, but her fingers were curled so tightly around the teacup they ached from the pressure.

Trey jerked as if she'd slapped him, his face paling while his eyes blazed a brighter blue. ''You don't want to marry me?'' he asked tightly.

''I didn't say that I don't want to marry you,'' Caitlin answered swiftly. ''Only that neither of us should feel compelled to marry the other. Any marriage is difficult, but forced marriages are doomed from the start.'' She waved a hand in the air for emphasis. ''I'm a living example of an unwanted child and an unhappy forced marriage.''

"But our baby isn't unwanted, Caitlin." Trey's deep voice held conviction.

Caitlin's heart clenched at the depth of emotion in his eyes. "Are you sure, Trey? You really want this baby?"

"Yes." Trey badly wanted to cross the space that separated them and hold her, but Sarah and Josh's presence kept him from moving. He glanced at Josh, then to Caitlin, frustrated.

"I think we should leave the two of you alone," Sarah said, reading the grim set of Trey's mouth.

"No. We can go to my place. Caitlin?"

Caitlin knew she needed to speak with Trey in private. But as she was about to agree, a wave of tiredness washed over her, accompanied by a repeat of the nausea and dizziness that had hit her earlier. Disoriented, she clutched the edge of the table and concentrated on breathing evenly, waiting till the uneasiness passed.

"Caitlin?" Trey's voice held panic. Two long strides brought him to the table. He squatted beside her, one hand on the back of the chair, the other resting on her jean-clad thigh. "Honey? Are you all right?"

Caitlin shuddered, swallowed and managed to nod. "Yes. I just feel queasy."

"Is it the baby? Should I get a doctor?"

"No, Trey. She just needs to lie down for a while." Sarah's calm voice reassured him. "She's suffering from morning sickness, that's all."

"Morning sickness?" Trey glanced at the clock on the stove. "It's almost noon. Is this normal?"

"Unfortunately, yes," Josh said dryly.

"I'll help her upstairs and tuck her back into bed." Sarah rose and stood behind Caitlin's chair.

"Can you walk?" Trey asked gently. "Why don't I carry you?"

"No, I…I'm sure I can walk."

Caitlin stood, swaying for a moment. Trey made a rough noise and rose swiftly, then bent and swung her off her feet and into his arms. She gasped and caught the edge of his jacket in a tight grip, turning her face into the warm curve of his throat.

"I'll turn the bed down." Sarah held the kitchen door for them and hurried up the stairs.

Trey didn't say a word as he strode through the house, up the stairway and down the hall into Caitlin's bedroom. He lowered her carefully to the bed, his hands fisted on the sheets beside her as he remained bent over her. She opened her eyes and looked at him, her face pale against the lace-edged white pillow slip.

"Are you all right?" he asked.

"I'll be fine," she whispered, wetting her dry lips with the tip of her tongue. "I feel awful, but Sarah assures me that this is perfectly normal and will pass." She smoothed a hand over her belly and managed a small smile. "I don't think he liked toast for breakfast."

Trey covered her hand with his. "Do you think it's a boy?" His voice rasped with emotion.

"I don't know, but I've been thinking of the baby as he. Do you want a boy?"

Trey took in her pale face and the faint dark smudges beneath her eyes. "I don't care, honey, as long as his mommy's okay and he's healthy." Tears welled in Caitlin's green eyes, and he brushed his lips against her eyelids, closing them. "You go to sleep," he said huskily. "I'll grill some steaks for us tonight at my place. We can talk about it then."

Caitlin nodded, too exhausted to reply.

Trey straightened and left the room. Sarah followed, pulling the door nearly closed behind them.

They returned to the kitchen in silence.

"Are you sure it's normal for her to be so ill?" Trey asked, worry darkening his voice.

"Yes, I'm sure."

"But it happened so fast. One minute she seemed fine, and the next she was pale, and I was sure she was going to faint."

"I know, but she should be past the worst of it in a few weeks."

"I hope so." Trey was unconvinced. He didn't remember Sarah and Jennifer during the early days of their pregnancies, and he had no experience with other pregnant women.

His worry over Caitlin was replaced by a more immediate problem. Josh had acted as Caitlin's surrogate father since he'd married Sarah when Caitlin was twelve. It didn't matter that Trey was thirty-six and Caitlin twenty-eight and that they were both well past the age of consent. Trey squared his shoulders and braced himself for the dressing-down he would endure only because of his respect for Josh and the love Caitlin bore for her uncle.

Strangely enough, Josh Hightower didn't seem angry. He leaned against the counter by the sink, his arms folded over his chest, his gaze thoughtful as he watched Trey.

"I'll take care of her, Josh."

"I know you will, Trey. It never occurred to me that you wouldn't." Josh's tone was mild, his gaze keen. "I have to admit, my first instinct was to punch you and find my shotgun, but I had time to think about it while you were upstairs. And it occurs to me—it's mighty strange that two people as smart as you and Caitlin got caught in this position."

Trey felt heat move up his throat and spread across his cheeks. How the hell was he supposed to explain to Caitlin's adoptive parents that she'd always made him so wild he could barely remember his name when he was with her, let alone remember to always use protection?

"It almost makes a man wonder if you wanted this to happen," Josh continued when Trey didn't respond.

Trey narrowed his eyes, his muscles tensing. "You think I got her pregnant on purpose so she'd have to marry me?" he asked, his voice raw. "You think I planned to ruin her life?"

"What makes you think you've ruined her life?" Sarah's voice was calm, reasonable.

"Being pregnant takes away her choices," he said

bleakly. "And we all know she made her choices about what she wanted to do with her life and where she wanted to live—and they don't include being married to me and living on a ranch in Montana." A swift image of Caitlin, dressed in a navy linen suit and seated against the backdrop of a quietly expensive Seattle restaurant, flashed through his mind.

"I wasn't aware that you'd asked Caitlin to marry you and she refused," Sarah said.

"She didn't refuse me. I never asked her."

"Then her choices never included the possibility of marriage to you and a life in Montana," Josh pointed out reasonably.

"She never would have considered me. You've visited her in Seattle—damn it, she's a university professor." Trey gestured, the sweep of his hand taking in his boots, his faded jeans, the denim jacket he wore and the world of buttes, pastures and prairie visible outside the kitchen windows. "I can't offer her a career that would replace the university nor a life that includes her choice of the ballet or symphony every night."

"Maybe that's not what she wants."

"She loves all that stuff," Trey said grimly. "She'd never willingly give it up to nurse colts and slog through mud in the spring and snow in the winter."

"I think you're selling her short, Trey. Are you forgetting how much she loved caring for calves and foals all the years she lived with us? And Caitlin loves winter." Sarah shook her head. "I know she loves living in Seattle, but given the choice, I'm not convinced that she would choose the city over ranch life.''

''Whether she would or wouldn't isn't relevant anymore.'' Trey's eyes were bleak. ''She no longer has a choice, and that's my fault. If I'd been more careful...'' He shook off the deep sense of guilt and regret, tugged the brim of his Stetson over his brow and moved toward the back door. ''When she wakes, tell her I'll be back around six, will you?''

''Sure,'' Josh said gently.

Trey spent the hours after leaving the Hightower spread struggling to cope with too many emotions. The sheer wonder that he was going to be a father warred with anger and hurt that Caitlin had chosen to tell her aunt Sarah before confiding in him. Simmering beneath the surface was a consuming guilt that his carelessness had caused Caitlin's life to be irrevocably changed. If there was also elation that her pregnancy left only one option—marriage—Trey didn't acknowledge it. One idea, however, he was absolutely clear about—Caitlin would marry him, and they would raise this child together. He'd grown up without a father. He was determined that his son or daughter would not suffer the same fate.

Caitlin dressed carefully for dinner with Trey. She chose a cream wool sweater dress with long sleeves and a modest scoop neck. The soft angora covered her from collarbones to wrists, the hem falling below her knee. She felt shielded in the warm wool. She paired the dress with cream-colored alligator heels, a single gold chain and matching hoop earrings. After twisting to check the back of her dress in the mirror, she ran the brush through her hair one more time.

"Caitlin?" Sarah's voice carried easily up the stairway. "Trey's here."

"I'll be right down," she called, facing the mirror one last time. Her reflection was calm, without a hair out of place or a wrinkle in the soft dress. But her green eyes were shadowed, her cheeks too pale. Caitlin drew a deep breath, collected her purse from atop the dressing table and left the room. Max woke from his half sleep atop the bedspread and leaped from the bed to follow her.

Trey waited at the bottom of the stairway, still wearing his hat, his jacket unbuttoned over black slacks and a pale blue fine cotton shirt. Caitlin's footsteps on the stairs distracted him from his conversation with Sarah, and his head turned quickly, his gaze finding her with swift sureness. She paused on the bottom step, her eyes nearly level with his.

"There you are, Caitlin," Sarah said. "Have a nice evening, you two. I've got pasta water that's going to boil over if I don't scoot." Sarah touched Caitlin's hand where it rested on the banister and hurried down the hall toward the kitchen.

Trey scanned Caitlin's face, the tenseness easing from his body as he realized that except for cheeks that were slightly paler than usual, she seemed to have fully recovered from her earlier distress.

"You look better than you did this morning," he commented. "How are you feeling?"

"Much better, thank you."

"Good." He took her long wool coat from her arm and held it for her. "Do you think you can eat something besides tea and crackers?"

Caitlin descended the last step and slipped her arms into the coat sleeves. His hands lingered on her shoulders and she caught her breath before she took a small step away. His fingers slid from her shoulders as she turned to face him. "Yes, I think so," she answered, surprised. "Actually, I'm starved."

"That's a relief. I wasn't sure if you'd be able to look at food, but just in case, there's a steak with your name on it in my refrigerator," he said, opening the door.

The October air was chilly, and Caitlin tucked her chin into her coat collar as they walked toward Trey's truck. He reached around her and pulled open the passenger door, his hand cupping her elbow as she stepped in. He leaned closer, carefully tucking her coat inside. For a moment, he was so near that she breathed in the scent of familiar aftershave and warm male, but then he shifted and shut the door, closing her into the warm interior. He strode around the cab and pulled open the driver's side door, slid behind the steering wheel and pulled the door shut, closing out the cold rush of air.

He twisted the key in the ignition, and the engine growled to life. He let it idle in neutral while he half-turned to look at her, his forearm resting on the curve of the steering wheel, his other arm along the seat back.

"Are you okay with having dinner at the house?" he asked softly, searching her face. Though dusk had long ago fallen, the soft glow of the dash lights enabled him to see her expression. "We could eat at a restaurant if you'd rather, but I thought our discussion would be better held in private."

She looked at him for a long moment, weighing her choices.

"I think I'd be more comfortable talking about the baby in private," she said finally, choosing privacy over the danger of being alone with him.

"All right." He shifted the truck into gear.

Conversation was nonexistent, each of them wrapped in their own thoughts until they reached Trey's ranch buildings. He parked in front of the house and took Caitlin's elbow once again to help her alight from the big truck, not releasing her as they hurried up the sidewalk to the porch, the cold wind brisk at their backs. He shoved open the door and ushered her inside, closing the door quickly behind them.

"Brrr." Caitlin shivered and rubbed her arms. "The nights are definitely getting colder."

"Yeah. Winter's not far off. Here, let me take your coat."

Caitlin slipped her arms from the black wool overcoat. Trey's dog, Chukka, chose that moment to enter the room, yawning wide and stretching before padding closer to sniff at her skirt.

"Well, hello there." Caitlin bent at the waist and smoothed her palm over his head, petting the silky black fur of his ears. His tongue lolled, his eyes half-closed with pleasure. She laughed softly and looked at Trey. "How did you get one of Jennifer's babies?"

Trey hung his hat and coat beside hers and clicked the closet door shut. "I lived with Jennifer and Lucas while I was building this house. The little fella started following me around and insisted on sleeping in my room at night, so Jennifer decided that he'd chosen me as his owner. When I moved in here, Chukka came with me."

"I've always wondered how this guy got the name Chukka when most of Jennifer's dogs were named after characters in fairy tales. Did she tell you?"

"Not exactly, but I know that Jennifer let Alexie name all of the puppies in the litter when he was born."

"Where did Alexie find the name Chukka?"

"I don't know." Trey shrugged. "You know Alexie. I'm sure she has a perfectly reasonable explanation, but I've never asked her."

"Hmm." Caitlin straightened and glanced around the room. Polished wood floors gleamed like satin. The golden sheen of oak flooring was repeated in the custom bookshelves that covered one entire wall, the shelves crammed from floor to ceiling with books and state-of-the-art video and stereo equipment. Furniture was sparse. Only a deep-brown leather sofa and matching massive armchair were in the room, a brass floor lamp standing between them, a plush Oriental wool rug covering the floor in front of the sofa and chair.

"Oh, Trey." Her voice was soft with delight. "This is really lovely. Did you design the house yourself?"

"Yes." A deep rush of pleasure flooded him. He wanted her to like his home. He'd labored long hours building it, pouring his heart and soul into the project. "And built it myself. I hammered nearly every nail, with help from Lucas and Josh and the rest of the family."

Caitlin moved farther into the room, stopping to look at the jewel colors and the pattern of the Oriental rug. "This is beautiful."

Hands tucked into his slacks pockets, Trey followed her. "I picked it up in Pakistan."

"Really?" Caitlin glanced at him, struck anew with how little she knew of his life in the years they'd been apart. A collection of South American pottery caught her eye, and she strolled to the long shelves. The pottery sat on an oak shelf next to a carved bookend that secured several leather-bound books. "And these?" she asked, fascinated by the muted colors and the exotic designs of the squat earthenware.

"Colombia."

She trailed a finger down the aged leather spine of one of the books, tilting her head to read the title. Startled, she glanced at Trey, her eyes wide with disbelief. "This can't be a first edition of *David Copperfield*—is it?"

"Yes, it is."

"Where in the world did you get it?"

Trey shrugged. "A family gave it to me."

"Gave it to you!" She stared at him in shock before her eyes narrowed suspiciously. "What did you do for the family?"

"Nothing much." She clearly didn't believe him, because she crossed her arms and lifted an eyebrow expectantly. Trey frowned, but she didn't relent. "The family was cooperating with U.S. authorities in Central America when their only son was kidnapped by a drug cartel. I was assigned to locate him and bring him out of the jungle." He gestured toward the rare book. "I knew the family before the kidnapping and the father and I shared an interest in rare books. When I refused to accept the reward money, he sent me the book."

"Ah." Caitlin glanced at the book again. "The kidnapping—was that when you injured your leg?"

"Yeah." Trey waited for her to ask another question. In Seattle, she'd asked him where he'd gotten the angry scar on his thigh, and he'd told her only that he'd been wounded in Central America and the disabling injury had cost him his eighteen-year career in the military. But passion hadn't allowed a lot of time for conversation, and he'd quickly distracted them both.

"Do you miss it? The traveling, the excitement, the danger?" she asked, curious.

"No." His answer was swift, decisive. "I'm more than ready to settle in Butte Creek and be a full-time rancher. The only regret I have is that I didn't finish a full twenty years. Although, to tell you the truth, I never started out to serve twenty years in the military. It just turned out that way."

"Mm." Caitlin nodded, distracted by the offhand description of a life-and-death incident that Trey clearly considered just another day at work.

Trey was relieved that Caitlin didn't question him further. His glance followed hers around the living room. "I'm glad you like the house." He took her arm and walked her down the hall to the kitchen. "It's not big, but it's all mine."

His fingers left her arm and he gestured to the counter separating the kitchen from the dining area where a small table was neatly set for two.

"Have a seat." He pulled out one of the stools pushed under the wide counter and waited until she sat before moving around the counter and into the alley kitchen, folding the cuffs of his long shirt sleeves over his forearms as he walked.

Caitlin was fascinated by the unconscious ease with which he moved around the kitchen. He lifted the lid from a copper-bottomed saucepan on the stove and glanced inside before turning on the burner beneath. Then he collected two scrubbed baking potatoes from the counter and arranged them on a rack in the microwave. He closed the door and the oven beeped quietly in response as he set the timer before he took two steaks from the refrigerator and glanced at her.

"Do you still like your steak medium rare?"

"Yes, please."

He checked the broiler before slipping steaks and

pan onto the rack, then he pulled open the refrigerator door and collected two salad bowls. He walked past her to set the bowls on the table, glanced up, and caught her watching him. He halted in mid-stride, one eyebrow lifting inquiringly.

"What?"

"You're so good at this."

"This? What 'this'?"

Caitlin indicated the table behind him and the brightly lit kitchen. "Cooking—kitchen stuff."

Trey shrugged. "I wouldn't say I'm good at it, exactly. I learned enough to keep from starving if I didn't want to go out—or if there wasn't a restaurant near." He narrowed his eyes and strolled nearer. "How about you? Are you a gourmet cook, or do you slap together peanut-butter-and-jelly sandwiches for dinner?" His voice dropped an octave and went husky, quieter.

He bracketed her with his arms, his hands resting palms down on the countertop on either side of her. Caitlin tipped her head to meet his gaze. She was seated sideways on the stool, and her hip and left thigh were nudged by his denim-covered thighs, her shoulder and upper arm only a breath away from his chest.

"I like to cook, but I've been known to eat peanut butter and jelly on occasion, especially if I've worked late and haven't been to the grocery store for a while." Caitlin refused to be shaken by his nearness, but she was so vividly attuned to him that she unconsciously changed her breathing until the subtle shift brought her breathing into sync with his. Her gaze strayed over his face, noting the fine lines that radiated from the corners of his eyes, the gold-tipped brown lashes that were ridiculously long for a male, the polished sheen of his skin and the faint shadow of heavy gold beard beneath. His face was as familiar to her as her own, yet that of a stranger. The ten years they'd spent apart had matured him in both obvious and subtle ways. She wondered belatedly if he saw the same depth of change in her that she saw in him. Her gaze lifted to meet his, and she caught her breath. He was watching her, his blue eyes blazing with emotion.

"Trey." Her voice was a soft murmur. Her hand lifted of its own accord to cup his face, her fingers smoothing the skin. His powerful body went taut as a bowstring, his thigh muscles flexing against her hip.

He caught her hand in his and turned his face into her palm, closing his eyes, his expression tormented. For a long moment he stood perfectly still, then he drew a deep breath, pressed an openmouthed kiss against the soft skin of her palm and carefully placed her hand on the countertop.

"Later. I can't touch you now or we'll never get around to dinner, and you need to eat."

The words were sandpaper rough, growled as he stepped away from her. Caitlin realized that she'd nearly pushed them both beyond the boundaries she'd set. She thrust trembling fingers through her hair and tucked the loose strands behind her ears, staring at

Trey's back as he yanked open the oven door and removed the steaks.

"Can I do anything?" she asked.

"You can pour us something to drink."

She slid off the high stool, her legs unsteady, and crossed to the refrigerator. "What do you want?" she asked, peering inside.

"Whatever you're having is fine."

She glanced over her shoulder at him, meeting his gaze with a wry smile. "I'm drinking milk these days, Trey."

"That's fine with me."

"Are you sure? I don't mind if you have something else."

"Nope." He speared a steak and transferred it to a dinner plate. "Believe it or not, I usually drink milk with dinner." He caught her look of skepticism. "It's true. Didn't you notice the gallon of milk in the fridge?"

Caitlin took the plastic container off the cold shelf, nudged the door closed with her hip and walked to the little alcove that held the table. "Okay, you've convinced me." She filled glasses and went into the kitchen to return the milk container to the fridge. "Anything else I can do?"

"You can put the broccoli in a bowl—it's in the saucepan on top of the stove." Holding two dinner plates, with a steak and baked potato on each, Trey passed her on his way to the table.

While Caitlin scooped broccoli from pan to bowl, Trey lowered the lights in the dining area with a dimmer switch. And when Caitlin placed the bowl of broccoli on the table, he clicked off the kitchen lights.

He seated Caitlin before taking his own chair.

"Do you still like your baked potatoes with only salt and butter?" he asked as she shook out her napkin and laid it across her lap.

"I do—how did you remember that?" Surprised, she paused and stared at him.

"I remember everything about you."

Bemused, Caitlin stared at him.

He held her gaze for a long, taut moment before a brief smile eased the intensity from his face. "I thought you said you were starved?"

"I am." She looked at her plate, and her stomach chose that moment to rumble. Trey chuckled, and she glanced up quickly to find him smiling with amusement, all tension gone. She laughed and picked up her fork. "Tea and crackers obviously wasn't enough to keep my stomach satisfied today."

"Then I won't have slaved in the kitchen for nothing." He offered her the bowl of broccoli.

"A very healthy meal," she commented, accepting the bowl. "I'm impressed."

"Don't be," he said dryly. "The broccoli's for your benefit. I read somewhere that nutrition is important for pregnant ladies."

Caitlin's fork halted halfway to her mouth, and she slowly lowered it to her plate. A small frown created lines of worry between her brows. "Trey, I wanted to—"

"Don't. We'll talk about it after you've eaten."

She met his steady gaze and nodded slowly.

It wasn't until they'd finished eating, washed, dried and returned dishes to the cupboard and were sitting in the living room with cups of decaf that Trey broached the subject of the baby.

"Would you have told me you were pregnant if I hadn't overheard you and Sarah today?"

"Yes." Her feet tucked beneath her on the sofa, Caitlin met Trey's gaze with straightforward honesty. He sat forward in the overstuffed armchair, his forearms resting on his thighs, coffee cup cradled in his palms between his spread legs. "I would have. When I learned I was pregnant, I decided to take a leave of absence from teaching and come home to Montana to tell you about the baby. And to decide what to do."

"What to do?" He clenched his jaw, and his fingers tightened around his cup. "You're not considering getting rid of the baby, are you?"

"No." Her response was instant and firm. "Absolutely not. I want this baby, Trey. There is absolutely no possibility of choosing any other option." An awful thought occurred to her, and she stiffened. "You aren't suggesting that I not have the baby, are you?"

"No. Hell, no."

His affronted denial reassured her, and she relaxed, easing against the sofa cushions. "Good."

"What I'm suggesting is that we get married and make a home for our baby."

Caitlin sipped her coffee and eyed him over the rim of her cup before she shifted, her nylon-clad legs whispering softly as she swung her feet to the floor and sat erect. "I told you earlier, Trey, I'm not sure that we should be married."

His eyes narrowed. "Why not?"

"Because two people living in the same house only because one of them is pregnant is not necessarily a good thing. There needs to be more between a husband and wife than duty and obligation."

"There's more between us. We could start bonfires just by being in the same room together."

"Passion isn't enough, either. I know that we're compatible sexually—"

"We're more than compatible. What happens between us is rare. There's probably not one man and woman in a million who fit like we do."

"That's pheromones and biology—and that's not what I mean. There are other, deeper issues that hold two people together through good times and bad."

"Like what?"

"Like mutual goals and common values."

"Common values? I've not been celibate, but you'd never have to worry about me being unfaithful after we're married," he said bluntly. "As for mutual goals, you've got me there. I don't know how your having a career at the university is going to mesh with mine as a rancher, but we'll just have to work out a compromise of some sort."

"Marriages that last need to have honesty and commitment—and love."

"Hell." Trey thrust his fingers through his hair and shoved upright, pacing away from her across the floor. He should have known she'd want the words. He couldn't say them. Just the thought of what the words entailed made him break out in a cold sweat. "Most people claim they love each other when what they really mean is they want to go to bed together. That's lust, not love."

"That's not true of Josh and Sarah, nor Jennifer and Lucas."

"Maybe, but you're talking about four people out of—how many couples do you know? A dozen, two dozen, maybe a hundred?"

"There's also Zach and CeCe."

"All right, so we both know three couples who have found something special. Maybe they're the exceptions that prove the rule. Fifty percent of marriages in America end up in divorce court, and I'll bet you ten to one that every one of those people told each other that they were in love when they said 'I do.'"

Trey could tell by Caitlin's expression that she didn't agree with him, but he refused to lie to her. "I don't believe in love, Caitlin," he said flatly. "My mother told me she loved me every day, usually right before she left for a bar to spend the grocery money on booze. And she fell in love with a new man every Saturday night." He shook his head, his face grim. "Too many people say that word too often until it doesn't mean a thing. I don't believe in love. Hell, I'm not sure I even know what the word means. Do you?"

"I think so."

"Do you?" He halted and turned, hands on hips,

and stared at her. She looked every inch the professor—her spine straight, slender legs crossed one over the other at the knee, slim hands cradling her coffee cup in her lap, the cream angora dress ending a demure inch above her knees. Her green gaze held his with unswerving determination, demanding answers, giving not an inch. Caitlin Drummond was a woman sure of herself, intelligent, educated, with a self-possession that was damn near frightening. Not to mention impressive. How the hell was he going to convince her that she needed him? "Do you love the child you're carrying?"

Caitlin's palm instantly sought her midsection. "Yes. Yes, I do."

"Then how can you deny him the chance to have two parents to care for him?"

"Regardless of whether or not you and I are married, you would still have all the rights of a father," she protested. "I would never do anything to keep you from having a place in his life. I want this baby to have two parents who love him."

"And just how are you going to accomplish that if we don't live together? How will I spend time with him every day if I don't live in the same house?" He halted, a frown creasing his forehead. "For that matter, if we're not married, are we even going to be living in the same state? Are you staying in Montana after your leave of absence from the university, or are you going back to Seattle?"

"I haven't decided," she admitted.

"This won't work, Caitlin. I'll be damned if my

son or daughter will grow up without a father, and the only way we can accomplish that is if we're married.''

''I'm not convinced that marriage is the best solution.''

''It's the only solution.'' He squatted in front of her and took her hands, his gaze intense. ''I'm sorry that I didn't take better care of you, Caitlin, but I can't go back and undo what's been done. We're going to have a child together, and I want to do the right thing for you and the baby.''

Caitlin could have cried. She'd been so afraid that he would feel responsible for her pregnancy and feel compelled to marry her. His words confirmed that was exactly how he felt.

Trey read the swift rejection written on her face, and his heart sank. The depth of disappointment he felt staggered him. Before she could refuse him aloud, he stood and caught her hand in his. ''Don't say no. Not yet. Think about it.'' He took her cup and set it on the floor next to his, then took her hand and tugged her off the sofa. ''I want you to see the rest of the house.''

He slung an arm around her shoulders and tucked her against his side, their hips grazing as they walked from the living room into the hallway that ran from the front to the back of the house.

''This is the small bathroom.'' He pushed open the door and stepped inside, ushering Caitlin with him. The bathroom had white porcelain fixtures and an antique oak washstand converted to hold a modern sink. It was spotless and untouched. "I never use it."

He stepped out of the bathroom and pushed open the door to a bedroom across the hall. It held a spring and mattress, covered with sheets and blankets, on a low frame and no other furniture.

"This is the guest room—although no one's ever stayed here." He looked at her. "It's a nice size for a nursery, don't you think?"

Caitlin felt his gaze on her but didn't look up. Instead, she scanned the pale green carpet, the simple bed and the single large window, bare of curtains. "It's bigger than tract house guest rooms," she commented neutrally. "I like that."

She didn't say anything further, and Trey had to be satisfied.

He turned and guided her to the end of the hall.

"This is the master bedroom." He stepped inside and flicked the light switch. Lamps on each side of the king-size bed flooded the room with soft, golden light. It gleamed and warmed the blue of the bedspread and drapes that were pulled closed over the windows. "The bathroom is over here." He walked with Caitlin across the expanse of hardwood floor, their steps muffled as they crossed the deep pile of a vivid blue, cream and scarlet Oriental rug.

Once again, he flipped a wall switch, and Caitlin gasped. The bathroom was huge and boasted a sunken tub. Deep blue throw rugs matched the plush towels that hung askew on brass racks. Shaving gear cluttered the top of the sink cabinet, and the faint smell of his cologne lingered in the air.

The room was somehow deeply intimate, and Caitlin was submerged with the smells, the warmth of Trey's body along her side, his arm enclosing her, his palm resting on her shoulder, his fingers splayed over her collarbone. Behind them, the bedroom was silently seductive, the expanse of bed inviting.

"...a luxury but the jets in the tub work wonders when my leg acts up."

Caitlin was silent, unable to find her voice.

"Caitlin?"

He turned his head and looked at her, his eyes narrowing swiftly, heating as he stared at her. His gaze dropped to her mouth, fastened there with burning intensity when she dampened dry lips with the tip of her tongue.

Without thought, Trey claimed her mouth in a searing kiss.

Chapter Four

"Trey, I don't..."

Too late. Much too late to protest.

Trey's hand tightened on her shoulder, and his free hand slipped around her waist, easing her against him, breast to breast, thigh to thigh.

If he'd restrained her, she would have fought to escape. But he didn't. The loose clasp of his arms was just enough to keep her body resting lightly against his. And he kissed her with slow deliberation, breaking the seal of their mouths to brush his lips across the arch of her cheekbone, down the line of her jaw to the underside of her chin before he changed the angle of his head and sealed his mouth over hers once again.

Caitlin's good intentions flew out the window. She

exhaled a low sigh of need and surrender and slipped her arms around his neck to tug him closer. She arched against him in an unconscious plea, and he stroked his palms down her back from the nape of her neck to the curve of her bottom, his fingers pressing her against him in a rhythm that matched the slow movements of his tongue against hers.

Obeying an instinct as old as time, he walked her backward across the room and eased them onto the bed. Without taking his mouth from hers, he nudged her thighs apart and settled against her.

Caitlin nearly sobbed with relief at the heated weight of his body blanketing her, but the feel of his heavily muscled thigh as it wedged between hers set off alarm bells. Her fingers reluctantly left his hair and moved to his shoulders, her palms pushing against him.

His senses fogged with hunger, Trey slowly realized that Caitlin had stopped urging him closer. He lifted his mouth from hers and drew back a scant few inches, just far enough to look at her.

"What?" he whispered, distracted by the passion that flushed her cheeks and hazed the deep green of her eyes. He trailed his fingertips over the smooth arch of her eyebrow and down the heated silk of her cheek to the corner of her mouth. Her hair fanned in an ebony spill of silk against the deep blue bedspread.

"We can't do this," she murmured, her voice husky, regretful.

"Yes, we can."

"Well, I can't."

"Caitlin." The single word held a wealth of male frustration. He knew he could seduce her. But what about after? Would she trust him again?

"Trey, I don't want us to sleep together, and I can't do it without your cooperation."

Good. Because you're not getting it. "Why not?" he asked aloud.

"Because it's impossible for me to think clearly when we're making love. And we have important decisions to make. We have to be clearheaded and practical."

"Clearheaded and practical." He repeated the words, staring at her in disbelief. His gaze moved from her eyes to her mouth, lingered on the faintly swollen curve of her lower lip and moved to the soft angora that covered the peaks of her breasts. She was every bit as aroused as he was, yet she expected them both to be clearheaded. And practical. "I don't think that's possible."

"It has to be. It's going to take both our efforts to keep sex out of our relationship until we decide if we should marry."

"The decision to marry was made the day you became pregnant," he said implacably.

"No, it wasn't." Caitlin was determined. "I'm not convinced that you want me or our baby."

"I think it's obvious that I want you," he growled. "If I didn't, there damn sure wouldn't be a baby."

She stiffened under him, her eyes narrowing. "You know very well I'm not talking about lust."

He stared at her for a long moment, but her level

gaze never left his. He drew a deep breath and exhaled slowly, then he rolled away from her and stood, catching her hand to pull her upright.

"I think it's time I take you home."

Neither of them spoke during the drive from Trey's ranch to Caitlin's home. Silently he walked beside her as she climbed the steps to the porch of the dark, silent house, but when she reached for the doorknob, he stopped her with a hand on her arm.

She looked over her shoulder. Moonlight found its way beneath the porch overhang, the cool, silver light providing just enough illumination to allow her to see the emotion that roiled in the depths of Trey's eyes. Trapped by the complicated mix of heat and regret that shone there, she made no objection when he turned her and pulled her into his arms.

"I know this marriage isn't what you want," he said, his voice taut with restraint. "And for good reasons. You've spent years building a career and a life you love in the city. I've spent years traveling the world and learned that I want to live on a Montana ranch. How we'll resolve our life-styles baffles me. But an even bigger problem is that you're a woman who needs to know that the man she marries loves her—you need to hear the words. I wish I could give them to you, but I don't know anything about loving—not the kind you deserve—and I doubt whether I'm capable of learning. But I'll try. I want you and I want this baby. I promise I'll try my damnedest to make you happy.

"If you need more time to get used to the idea of being tied to me forever, then I have to accept that. I don't like it, and you know I'd rather we get married right away, but you have the right to make up your mind in your own time. All I ask is that while you're thinking about marrying me, you give me a chance to convince you that a marriage between us will work."

It was more than Caitlin had hoped for—and exactly what she wanted. She smiled with relief.

"Thank you, Trey." A thought occurred to her. "And you'll help me keep sex out of our relationship?"

He clenched his jaw and narrowed his eyes. Caitlin held her breath.

"I don't think it will work," he said flatly. "But I'll try—unless you tell me you want me." He pulled her into his arms and slid one hand into her hair, his fingers fisting in the heavy silk to tug her head back. Hard blue gaze met steady green. "And if you do, I'll take everything I can." His gaze flicked from her eyes to her mouth and back to meet her gaze. "You're mine, Caitlin. You have been since you were sixteen, and I'm damned tired of waiting for you."

Before Caitlin could assimilate the stunning declaration, his mouth took hers in a demanding kiss that stole her breath and left her aching when he released her. Then he reached behind her to shove open the door and gently moved her inside. Moments later, she stood staring dazedly at the closed door. The sound of his boots echoed softly across the porch boards before the low growl of a pickup engine turning over and the crunch of gravel under tires faded into the night, leaving the house quiet once again.

"Oh, my," she whispered, touching fingertips to lips still damp from the pressure of his. She turned and climbed slowly up the stairs to her bedroom, undressing without turning on the lamp before she climbed beneath the sheets and quilt to lie on her back, staring sightlessly at the white ceiling. *What did he mean that I've belonged to him since I was sixteen? Was it so obvious how I felt about him?*

Pondering the question brought no answers. Downstairs, the grandfather clock struck midnight, but Caitlin's churning thoughts continued to hold sleep at bay.

Trey was having even less luck falling asleep. He finally tossed back the tangled sheets and blankets and stalked down the hall to the kitchen to collect a soda from the refrigerator before returning to the bedroom to lean against the window frame and stare out at the dark landscape.

The view of the shadowy barn and buttes beyond gave way to a flood of memories.

He had a week's leave from the Army and looked forward to spending Christmas in Butte Creek. All holidays were cause for celebration at the Hightower ranch, but Christmas rated a dizzying round of neighborhood parties from the first week of December through New Year's Eve.

Standing with a cluster of neighboring ranchers, Trey cradled a glass of punch in one hand and listened as Josh described the difficulties he was having with a stubborn three-year-old stud. Around him, laughing, chattering guests thronged Lucas and Jennifer's long living room and spilled into the hallway and kitchen. Just behind him, a Christmas tree was strung with twinkling lights, its branches stretching upward to brush the ceiling. The evergreen's pungent scent blended with the aroma of bayberry candles and the more subtle smells of women's perfume and men's aftershave.

Surrounded by friends and the warm scents and sights of Christmas, Trey let the welcome ease and familiarity of family and home wash over him.

"Trey."

A hand closed over his forearm. Trey glanced over his shoulder and found Murphy Redman. Mischief gleamed in the older man's black eyes, and Trey was instantly suspicious.

"What's up, Murphy?"

"Zach needs to see you."

"Where is he?" Trey's gaze flicked over the room, but he couldn't locate the tall rancher in the laughing crowd.

"Over by the door. Come on."

Murphy kept a firm grip on Trey's arm as they crossed the packed room. A small cluster of people filled the wide entryway to the hall.

"Zach!" The husky feminine tone was half laughter, half plea. "Let me go!"

"Nope. And stop wiggling." Zach Colby's deep voice held amused determination.

"Here he is, Zach," Murphy declared, releasing Trey's arm.

The small gathering of people shifted and turned to face Trey, moving aside to form a semicircle around Zach. The tall rancher's gaze met Trey's over the head of the slim woman whose shoulders he held.

"It's about time, Trey," Zach complained good-naturedly. "I didn't know how much longer I could keep her from escaping." He spun the woman around and held her in front of him.

Trey's throat went dry. He knew that silky fall of ebony hair, the challenging stare from those green eyes, but the rest of her... His gaze moved swiftly from the crown of her head, over the lush curves outlined by the emerald green wool of her dress, down the length of slender legs to her feet and up again to her eyes. He hadn't seen Caitlin Drummond since his last furlough nearly two years before—and then she'd been a coltish, long-legged fourteen-year-old. She must be sixteen now. And all grown-up.

"Hello, Trey."

The greeting jerked him to awareness, and he wondered how long he'd been standing frozen, gaping at her. He glanced quickly at the faces around him and realized to his relief that they were all looking at Caitlin with varying degrees of amusement and expectation.

"What's going on?" He'd known Caitlin since she was twelve years old, so the swift lowering of her lashes, the small smile and quick glance she darted at Murphy told him volumes. He turned to look at Murphy and noticed the wide grin the silver-haired cowboy wore. "What did she do this time?"

"She tricked CeCe into standing under the mistletoe, then she maneuvered Zach into kissing her," Murphy said. "Before Zach and CeCe, it was me and Annabel."

"And I decided that what's good for the goose is good for the gander," Zach said mildly, easily restraining Caitlin when she wriggled in a bid for escape. He glanced above Trey's head and nodded. "You're under the mistletoe, and now it's Caitlin's turn to play the game."

Trey tilted his head and glanced upward. Sure enough a glittering gold satin ribbon and a fat green ball of mistletoe dangled from the doorjamb. He lowered his gaze to meet Caitlin's, anticipation curving his mouth upward in a slow smile.

"Sounds like a plan to me," he drawled. He shoved his half-empty glass of punch at Murphy. "Hold my glass, Murphy." He held out his arms. "Come here, pretty girl."

Caitlin's green eyes narrowed suspiciously, the smooth arch of her dark brows veeing downward in a frown. She stared at him for a long moment before she shrugged in acceptance. "All right. You win."

Zach released her, and she stepped forward, resting her hands on Trey's forearms for balance as she went up on tiptoe and brushed a quick kiss against his cheek before dropping onto her heels.

"There." She half-turned to look over her shoulder at Zach.

"You call that a kiss?" Trey didn't know what demon drove him. He only knew he wanted more than that all too brief touch of her lips against his skin. Much more. He slipped his arms around her waist and tugged her forward, closing the space between them until their bodies touched from breast to thigh. The swift move startled her, and she looked at him. Before she could protest, Trey bent his head and claimed her mouth.

The kiss was chaste, but the feel of her soft lips beneath his, the lush curves of her body resting lightly against him, the scent of perfumed skin and the silky brush of her hair against his cheek nearly stopped his heart. He wanted to hold her and explore the sweet lure of her heated mouth for hours. Only the whistles, clapping and shouts of approval from their friends made him realize that he had to let her go.

Reluctantly, he lifted his head and looked at her. His fingers tightened at her waist as he read the dazed wonder on her expressive face. He bent to kiss her again, but Murphy clapped a hand on his back, shaking him to awareness.

"Merry Christmas, Trey. Caitlin."

The older man pulled Caitlin away from Trey and dropped a kiss on her cheek before swinging her into Zach's arms. Zach brushed a kiss against her nose and shifted the laughing young woman into the arms of her uncle Lucas.

Relieved that the boisterous crowd was focused on

teasing Caitlin, Trey welcomed the breathing space to rally his composure.

She's only sixteen. Damn. Much too young for what he wanted from her.

He shouldered his way through the crowd and bypassed the punch for a shot of Jack Daniels.

Trey shook off the memories and took a long pull from the can of soda.

The rest of that week between Christmas and New Year's, he'd avoided Caitlin as much as possible. When his furlough ended, he was relieved to leave Butte Creek behind, thankful for the respite. His friends had teased him about the shock written on his face when he'd seen Caitlin and felt the kiss that followed, but he'd managed to smile easily and deny that she was anything more than the surrogate little sister she'd always been. Convincing *himself,* however, was another matter entirely. Even after he'd returned to duty, his slumber was destroyed by hot, restless dreams of the girl with mysterious green eyes.

She'd been too young for him at sixteen. But she was eighteen, just graduated from high school and more than old enough, when he was wounded in South America and sent home on leave to recuperate. Neither of them had been able to resist the power of the attraction that drew them together like lodestones after simmering unsatisfied for two years.

Choosing to be noble and leave her behind when he returned to active duty had left an aching hole inside him that had never been filled.

He never would have purposely gotten her pregnant to force her to marry him. But now that she was, he was fiercely glad that they'd been given a second chance.

Just how the hell I'm supposed to convince her to marry me is something I'd better figure out damned fast, he thought grimly.

He tossed the empty soda can into the wastebasket. The clatter startled Chukka, and he lifted his head, woofing questioningly.

''Go back to sleep, Chukka.'' The dog dropped his muzzle onto his paws, and Trey patted his head as he padded barefoot past him on his way to bed. He yanked the sheet and blankets into relative neatness and slid between them, only to toss and turn and gain little rest in the hours until morning.

Three days after sharing dinner with Trey, Caitlin slipped out of the house immediately after lunch. Although her grandmother and her aunts were immensely supportive and she loved them dearly, she needed a break from discussing her pregnancy.

Wrapped warmly in a flannel-lined jean jacket, her gloved hands tucked into its denim pockets and a bright green wool scarf around her throat, she paused by her open car door to tilt her head and inhale deeply. The October sun's rays held little warmth, and the brisk air carried a bite that warned of the winter to come. She scanned the sky and then the distant horizon, wondering if the clouds piled against the farthest buttes held snow. The thought that she'd still be in Butte Creek when winter blizzards arrived brought a smile to her face. Since returning to Montana, she'd become increasingly convinced that although she'd enjoyed her years in Seattle and the Pacific Northwest, she was ready to return permanently to the ranch country that she loved. She hadn't told her family she'd decided to stay in Butte Creek. She didn't want to compound the news of her pregnancy. But she was determined to find a way to use her assets, experience, training and resources to build a life for herself and her child in Montana…with Trey.

She refused to consider a future that didn't hold a family with Trey and their baby. The possibility that it might not was too painful to contemplate.

Which was why she was on her way to her great-uncle Wes's north pasture to visit her horses. She and her cousin J.J. had first learned of Wes's herd of quarter horses when they were children and came to the Drummond ranch to live. Caitlin had shared Wes's love of the herd, and he'd promised the horses to Caitlin as a dowry for her children. Each time she returned to Butte Creek, she visited the growing number of mares and their babies and brought home the gelding she'd raised from a colt to ride during her stay. The horses were an unbreakable bond between her and her great-uncle, and they dreamed and planned, carefully selecting stallions and breeding mares to develop the herd.

The rumble of an engine interrupted her musings, and Caitlin paused to glance down the lane. The sight of the familiar black pickup and its driver had her heart beating a little faster and her fingers closing tightly over the door frame. The truck came closer and slowed to a stop next to her.

"Hi." Trey took in her jacket, jeans and the open car door. "Going somewhere?"

"Yes."

He waited. She didn't elaborate. A wry smile tilted his mouth.

"Want to tell me where you're going?"

"No."

His gaze flicked from her stubborn chin to the house and the cars parked in front of the picket fence, then back to Caitlin. He shoved at the brim of his Stetson with one finger and grinned at her, his eyes lit with amusement. "Let me guess. Your grandmother is here, and you're escaping."

Caitlin felt her irritation easing away, and she smiled reluctantly. "You know us too well," she said wryly. She glanced from him to the ranch house. "I love her dearly, but..."

"But you're too independent to take well-meant advice easily." He finished the sentence for her.

She looked at him quickly, a sharp retort hovering on the tip of her tongue. But his blue eyes held affection and understanding without censure, and she nodded. "You're right, I'm afraid." She sighed. "Uncle Josh told me when I was a teenager that the reason Grandmother and I rub each other wrong on occasion is because we're equally stubborn."

Trey chuckled. "I suspect Josh is right."

Caitlin frowned and opened her car door farther.

''If you're looking for Josh, I think he's in the machine shop.''

''I'm not looking for Josh. I came to ask you to spend the afternoon with me.''

The fizz of excitement that his presence always generated licked along her veins. ''Really? Doing what?''

He shrugged. ''Whatever.'' He gestured toward the car. ''Where are you going?''

''To the north pasture to visit my horses.''

''Hop in. I'll take you.''

She eyed him assessingly.

''Don't be so suspicious,'' he said dryly. ''My truck won't have any problem with the potholes in the track across the pasture, but that low-slung car of yours is likely to get its muffler knocked off.''

''Hmm.'' Caitlin glanced at the inches between the ground and the shiny wax finish of her imported sedan and closed the door. Trey leaned across the seat and shoved the truck's passenger door open, and she climbed in beside him. ''Can we stop at the barn and pick up hay and oats and a salt block?''

''Sure. No problem.'' Trey shifted the truck into reverse and twisted to look out the rear window, one arm stretched along the seat as he backed the pickup to the barn door. He braked and looked at Caitlin when she reached for the door handle. ''I know where the feed is, Caitlin. I'll load it into the truck bed.''

''I can help,'' she insisted.

''No,'' he said quietly, his gaze holding hers. ''Humor me, okay. I don't want you lifting bales of hay or sacks of grain—not while you're pregnant.''

''All right.'' She might have protested, but the sincerity in his level gaze stopped her. She sat quietly, waiting while he exited the truck and loaded feed, the truck cab rocking gently as he tossed hay bales, a sack of oats and a salt block into the bed. She didn't doubt that he cared about the child she carried and she, too, had no wish to endanger the precious life inside her. *Maybe pregnancy is making me wiser,* she mused. *Didn't Aunt Sarah always tell me a smart woman picks her battles carefully because a truly wise woman accepts that she can't win them all?*

Trey slammed the truck's tailgate and returned to the cab.

''Do you want to go the long way around, or shall we cut across the pastures?''

''Cut across the pastures,'' Caitlin answered promptly.

''All right.'' Trey shifted into first gear and drove around the barn to a lane that paralleled the fence line. He eased the truck in and out of potholes. Caitlin bounced and grabbed the edge of the seat. ''You should buckle up, then you won't bounce around so much.''

''But I'll just have to unbuckle again when we get to the gates,'' she reminded him.

''Geez, woman,'' he growled without heat. ''I suppose that means you want me to open and close all the gates?''

''No.'' The slow, teasing grin he slanted at her

stirred little flickers of heat through her veins. Caitlin felt her face warm. ''I'm the passenger. You're the driver. I'll open and close the gates.''

''Tell you what,'' he offered. ''I'll open and close all the gates—for a price.''

She eyed him suspiciously. ''What's the price?''

''Each gate I get for you, you give me a kiss.''

''I don't think so, Weber. There must be six gates between here and Uncle Wes's north pasture.''

''Too many, huh?'' He narrowed his eyes and nodded judiciously.

''All right. Three kisses and three hugs—that's my best offer.''

Caitlin laughed. ''Your best offer? I'm not sure you're trustworthy.''

The look he gave her was pure innocence. ''Me? Not trustworthy? How can you say that?''

''Easy,'' she said dryly. ''I remember lying on your bed.''

The laughter in his blue gaze was swiftly replaced by dark fire. ''So do I.''

Caitlin swallowed convulsively, reminded all too vividly that she'd barely been able to summon the strength to stop him. He could have easily seduced her. She knew he could do it again in a heartbeat. She also knew that Trey had promised not to, and he wasn't a man to break his word.

He'd promised not to seduce her—unless she asked him to.

''All right,'' she said, her voice husky. ''Three kisses and three hugs.''

"Deal." Eyes on the lane ahead, he held out his hand, palm up.

"Deal." Caitlin lightly slapped his hand with hers.

Trey stopped at the first gate and shifted into neutral, set the brake, pushed open the door and stepped out, leaving the truck idling and the door open.

Caitlin watched him unlatch the steel gate hung between two sturdy metal posts and swing it wide. He loped to the truck, climbed inside and drove the truck through. Then he stepped out and jogged to close the gate. When he returned to the truck and slid behind the wheel, Caitlin eyed him warily.

He leaned toward her and unbuckled her seat belt.

"I thought the whole purpose of this was so I didn't have to unbuckle at every stop," she commented, her gaze on his sun-darkened, work-roughened fingers as they dealt easily with the latch.

"It is," he answered, lifting his head to look at her. He eased the belt away from her and braced one hand against the window, bracketing her with his body. "You don't have to deal with it. I will."

"Ah, I see." Her voice was a throaty murmur. He was so close that his breath stirred her hair where it brushed her cheek. Beneath the brim of his Stetson, his eyes were dark. "So..." She managed to get a word out, her throat dry, voice hushed. "Which will it be, a hug or a kiss."

Staring at his mouth, she watched in fascination as he smiled slowly, giving her a tantalizing glimpse of white teeth.

"Oh, a kiss, I think."

She waited breathlessly, but he didn't move closer. Her gaze left his mouth and moved upward to meet his questioningly.

"Our deal was that you give me a kiss for each gate I open." His level gaze met hers.

Suddenly, Caitlin understood. Lurking behind the noncommittal expression was a hint of vulnerability. He wouldn't forcibly take what she didn't want to give.

Was it any wonder she loved this man, she thought.

"*Give* being the operative word, I assume?" she asked unsteadily.

"Yeah," he said, his voice a deep rasp.

Caitlin leaned toward him, cradling his face in her palms. She brushed her mouth against his once, twice, before her lips settled against the tantalizing warmth of his. Bound only by the press of mouth to mouth, Caitlin kissed him endlessly. He didn't wrap her in his arms and pull her closer, but she was aware that his body was strung taut, the muscles in his arms corded with tension.

When at last she pulled away from him in order to breathe, his cheekbones were flushed, his nostrils flared, and his blue eyes were nearly black with tightly reined desire. Wordlessly, he fastened her seat belt and shifted beneath the steering wheel.

Caitlin drew in several deep breaths while she watched the hard muscles of Trey's thigh flex when he depressed the clutch and shifted, sending the truck forward across the pasture.

"So," she said into the pulsing silence. "One down, five to go."

He glanced sideways at her, and she shivered at the heat that blazed from his eyes.

"If I live that long," he muttered.

When he reached for her seat belt after the second gate, anticipation curled in her stomach.

"And this time?" she asked him. "Kisses or hugs?"

"Hugs," he said as he moved the belt aside. His jacket was already open, but he methodically unbuttoned her jean jacket from top to bottom and spread it wide. Then he caught her by the waist and picked her up, turning her so that she lay across his lap. "Put your arms around me."

Caitlin slipped her hands under his jacket and hugged him. The movement pressed her breasts against his chest, her hip against the buttons of his jeans.

Trey closed his eyes and nearly groaned aloud with pleasure and arousal. The soft silk of her hair brushed the underside of his chin, and he buried his nose and lips against the fragrant softness. He tangled the fingers of his right hand in her hair, sifting through the ebony strands to the silky ends.

Long minutes went by while he luxuriated in the sheer pleasure of holding her close. Then he reluctantly shifted her to her seat and carefully fastened her seat belt. One swift glance at her flushed face and arousal-hazed green eyes was enough to tell him that she wasn't immune to their closeness. He'd given his word that he wouldn't seduce her, but the physical pleasure they found together was a powerful inducement, and he wasn't averse to using any weapon at hand to convince her to marry him.

By the time Trey approached the last gate that barred their entrance to Wes Hildebrandt's north pasture, Caitlin was thankful she didn't have to open gates. She wasn't at all sure her legs would have held her after the shattering kiss she'd shared with Trey at the fifth gate.

The windmill and watering tank came into view, and she sat up straight, eager for a glimpse of the horses. A herd of mares and half-grown colts milled around the tank, and Caitlin frowned, leaning forward to peer intently out the windshield.

"Trey, isn't that someone riding Christmas Girl?"

He braked in front of the gate and followed her pointing finger.

"Yeah, I think so. Too little to be an adult, but what would a kid be doing this far from the ranch?"

He opened the gate, drove through, closed it and returned to the truck.

"I'll take a rain check on that hug you owe me, honey. I want to find out what the hell that kid's doing out here."

The truck moved slowly over the rough pasture, but the herd continued to drink and graze without reaction until the sorrel mare with the young rider on its back lifted its head, ears pricking alertly. The rider glanced around and stiffened.

Caitlin caught a swift glimpse of the child's face

and thin body clothed in a too-big tattered jacket, shirt, jeans and baseball cap before the trespasser dug heels into the sorrel's sides and urged the quarter horse into a run. Horse and rider raced away from the herd and the approaching truck, straight as an arrow to the distant fence line where a saddled horse stood patiently, head down, tied to the far side of the barbed wire fence.

"Damn." Trey whistled softly. "Can that kid ride. He hasn't even got a bridle or saddle on that mare."

Caitlin nodded silently, struck by the lines of horse and human blurring into one smooth being.

"Can we catch him?" she asked.

Trey shook his head. "Not a chance. By the time we could get the gate open and drive around, the kid would be long gone. I wonder who he is."

"I don't have a clue."

The rider pulled up the mare with small hands twisted in the horse's rough mane and slid off, slipping quickly through the strands of barbed wire. One of the barbs caught in the baseball cap and tugged it off. Carroty red hair tumbled to the child's shoulders. The girl ripped the hat free, jammed it on her head and mounted the saddled horse. A moment later, horse and rider were gone, disappearing over the rise of a small butte into the pasture beyond. Caitlin exhaled and only then realized she'd been holding her breath while she watched the child. She glanced at Trey. "You didn't recognize her?"

"Nope. I don't think I've seen her before. We can

ask your aunts and check with Annabel. They know most of the kids on neighboring ranches.''

He backed the truck up to the long wooden trough and hayrack just beyond the water tank and turned off the engine. Caitlin swung eagerly out of the cab and climbed into the bed of the pickup where she could observe the horses as they milled around the black truck.

Trey slapped horses on their haunches and shouldered them out of the way to reach the back of the truck. He released the latch and dropped the tailgate, then levered himself into the bed with Caitlin.

He pulled on work gloves and took a knife from his pocket, then bent to cut the twine from the hay bales before he broke one into flakes. He threw several flakes onto the ground, and the horses moved away from the truck and the feeders. While the animals were occupied, he broke the rest of the bales into flakes and tossed them into the hayrack. Then he leaped to the ground, shouldered the bag of oats and walked to the long trough. He slit open the bag, upended it and walked along the wooden feeder while he trailed oats into its length. He'd nearly finished when one of the mares realized what he was doing and trotted close to drop her muzzle into the grain. The rest of the herd followed, and Trey rejoined Caitlin, swinging up to sit on the lowered tailgate next to her and watch the mares and last spring's half-grown colts and fillies jostle for position at the grain.

''They look wonderful, don't they?'' Caitlin searched the herd for any sign of illness or trouble, but found only bright eyes and padded bodies blanketed with thick winter coats.

"They seem healthy," Trey agreed. He scanned the horses as they kept jostling and bumping each other for a turn at the grain. "Will Wes winter them over in this pasture?"

"He does sometimes, but I'd like to move them closer to home so we can monitor them more closely this winter," she murmured.

Trey glanced sharply at her, but her attention was clearly focused on the horses. *She'd like to move them? Does that mean she plans to be here all winter?*

"Oh, look," she said, delighted. "There's Sasquatch."

Diverted, Trey followed her pointing finger and found the black gelding she'd raised from a colt. He shook his head in disgust. "Damned if I can figure out why you gave that poor horse that god-awful name."

"Sasquatch fit him perfectly when he was a yearling. He hadn't shed his winter coat the first time I saw him, and he was shaggy and sweet."

Trey looked at her and rolled his eyes, then he slipped off the tailgate and picked up the block of salt. "Let's see if Sasquatch wants some salt."

He worked his way through the herd to the gelding and rubbed the animal's nose before letting him sniff the block of salt. The horse's ears swiveled forward, and his eyes lit with interest. He followed Trey out of the throng and bent his head to lick the block when Trey set it in the wooden holder.

Trey worked his way to Caitlin. ''He likes it,'' he commented, leaning his hips against the gate next to her knees. Arms crossed over his chest, he continued to scan the shifting herd for any sign of problems. The horses finished the oats and the compact circle shifted, dispersing as some of the horses moved to the hayrack, some to the water trough, some to the new salt lick and some to graze on the sparse, brown grass beyond the trampled dirt around the water tank.

Caitlin stirred beside him.

''Ready to take a closer look?'' he asked. She nodded, and before she could jump to the ground, he caught her at the waist and swung her from the truck.

''Thanks.'' She tugged her jacket down and brushed off the back of her jeans.

''No problem. Any excuse to get my hands on you is a pleasure,'' he drawled. ''Want some help with that?''

She looked at him. His gaze was fastened intently on the movements of her hands as she brushed off the seat of her jeans.

''No, thanks,'' she said with asperity.

His gaze flicked to meet hers, and his mouth lifted in a slow smile.

He has a beautiful mouth, she thought, *and I still owe him a kiss.* The thought was unsettling, and she looked away from him, moving to the nearest horse.

Trey followed her as she moved through the herd, petting and murmuring to her horses while she ran her hands over them, checking for any unseen lumps or untreated scrapes. She'd always been good with horses. He'd forgotten how much she loved them. In the years she'd lived in Seattle, he'd grown used to thinking of her in a suit standing center stage in a crowded lecture hall. He wanted to believe that Caitlin might be happy living in Montana so badly that it was painful.

It was more than an hour before Caitlin was satisfied that her beloved horses were happy and well. The late afternoon sun had lost what little heat it had held earlier, and Caitlin tucked her hands into her pockets and shivered, looking past Trey's shoulder to the lowering sun.

"I better be getting home, Trey. Grandmother is staying for dinner, and I should help Sarah."

"All right." He cupped her elbow and turned her toward the truck. "If I begged, do you think Sarah would ask me to stay for dinner, too?"

Caitlin laughed. "You know very well you wouldn't have to beg. My aunt Sarah would feed you every night of the week if she thought you would come."

"I know." Trey pulled open the truck door and lifted her inside.

He rounded the hood and slid beneath the wheel. The well-tuned engine turned over with a muted roar, and he eased the truck over the hillocks and holes of the pasture to the gate, where he shifted the transmission into neutral and set the brake.

Caitlin's heart hesitated and sped faster when he turned toward her. He draped one arm over the top of the steering wheel and with purposeful movements removed his Stetson and set it on the dash without taking his gaze from hers.

"You still owe me for that last gate."

Though Caitlin knew that any kiss, any touch would lead them down a path she wanted to avoid, she could hardly wait to respond to Trey's challenge.

Chapter Five

"That's right. I'd forgotten," she lied. "A hug, right?"

"Right."

With the same deliberation he'd shown before, Trey released her seat belt and unbuttoned her jacket before he picked her up and settled her across his thighs to face him.

Caitlin slipped her arms around his waist and stroked her palms up the muscled plane of his back. He responded by tightening the circle of his arms, his hands echoing the movements of hers as they smoothed her back over the soft denim of her jacket. She sighed silently and rested against him, tucking her head beneath his chin, her face nestled against his warm throat. She'd never felt this overwhelming sense of rightness and belonging with anyone else. Only with Trey had she ever felt complete and somehow whole.

"Earlier, when I asked you about leaving the horses in the pasture, you said you'd like to bring them closer to home this winter," Trey said. "Is Wes going to monitor them, or are you planning to be around all winter?"

"I want to monitor them myself," Caitlin said.

"So you're staying in Montana longer than Christmas?"

"Yes."

"How long?"

"Forever. I've decided to move back to Butte Creek permanently."

Trey stiffened. He tilted his head to look at her. *Does this mean that she's decided to marry me?* "What about your job?" he asked carefully, wary of reading too much into her decision to choose Butte Creek over Seattle.

"I've decided to resign from the university."

"But I thought you loved teaching?"

"I do. But just because I'm not teaching at the University of Washington doesn't mean that I can't remain in education. It's just a question of finding the right venue."

"Hmm. What about the baby?"

"What about the baby?"

"You know. Prenatal care, a good doctor, the hospital—all that stuff."

Caitlin chuckled. "I can use Dr. Johnson. He delivered Sarah, Jennifer and CeCe's babies, and he was my GP when I was a girl. I'm perfectly comfortable with him, and with the delivery room facilities at Butte Creek Hospital.''

Trey cautiously acknowledged the relieved delight that bubbled in his veins. ''Does your decision to stay in Montana mean you've made up your mind about marrying me?''

''No.'' Caitlin instinctively smoothed her fingertips over the worry creases on his forehead. ''But I'm determined to stay in Butte Creek, regardless of whether or not we marry. I don't want our child to grow up several states away and only able to visit his father and the rest of my family on summer vacations.''

Trey's inclination was to argue with her, but the knowledge that he wasn't racing against a time limit was an enormous relief. He gathered her closer against him, and she didn't protest the warm embrace.

''What about doctor's visits?'' he asked, his deep voice breaking the silence.

''What about them?''

''I want to go with you. You told me you wouldn't deny me access to our baby.''

''I meant after he's born.''

''The books say it's important for the parents to talk to the baby before birth.''

''Books?'' Caitlin lifted her head and gazed at him, her eyes widening at the flush of color that swept his cheeks beneath his tan. ''You're reading books about pregnancy and childbirth?''

''What's wrong with that?'' he asked defensively.

''Nothing,'' she said faintly. ''Not a thing.''

''Right, not a damned thing. So let me know when you have a doctor's appointment, and I'll drive you.''

''All right.''

Trey had been prepared for arguments, so her easy consent threw him off stride for a moment.

''Good. That's settled then.'' Encouraged by her willingness to allow him a claim on her and the baby, Trey stroked his palm over the silky crown of her head, fighting against the urge to kiss her while he thought about her pregnancy. ''Are you still suffering from morning sickness?''

She sighed regretfully. ''Yes, unfortunately.''

''Have you talked to a doctor about it? How much longer will it last?''

''Sarah assures me that I probably won't have it much longer. And no, I haven't seen Dr. Johnson yet, so I haven't asked him about the nausea. Let alone the rest of it,'' she added, almost to herself.

But Trey heard her offhand remark and tilted her face to his. ''What rest of it?'' he demanded, his gaze sharpening over her face.

''Just the usual pregnancy stuff,'' she said evasively.

He frowned. ''What usual pregnancy stuff?''

''Nothing for you to worry about.''

''Let me be the judge of what I should worry about. What other stuff?''

Caitlin looked away from him. ''My breasts are swollen—and they hurt.''

Without considering the consequences, Trey

brushed the tips of his fingers across the swell of her breast in a gentle, careful gesture of sympathy and concern. "Is that normal?"

Caitlin gasped softly. Not only were her breasts swollen, they were incredibly sensitive. The touch of his fingers sent a shaft of desire arrowing straight to her core. Stunned by the tidal wave of need that hit her, she caught his fingers.

Trey heard the swift intake of her breath. But it wasn't pain he read in the depths of her eyes, it was heat and desire. Trapped beneath hers, his fingers froze against the swell of her breast.

"Is it painful being touched?"

"No, not painful, but they're very sensitive." Her voice was a shaky whisper.

"I want to see you."

His expression was fierce, the tanned skin drawn taut over the hard bones of his face. His fingers were motionless, tensed over the top button of her shirt, waiting.

"You promised you wouldn't seduce me," she reminded him, her voice hushed.

"I won't. I want to see what carrying my baby is doing to your body."

She knew she should refuse him. But she couldn't deny the intensity in his eyes. Slowly, she took her hand from his. He lowered his lashes, his gaze intent on the small white buttons as he slipped them free and watched the gap widen between the edges of the shirt. He reached the waistband of her jeans and tugged gently, freeing the hem until he could slip the last button loose and slowly ease the shirt away from her body.

Caitlin's heart shuddered, her heartbeat a deep, pulsing throb that grew heavier when his fingers unhooked the front clasp of her bra. His hands were dark and very male against the smooth, pale skin of her breast as he pushed the cream satin and lace cups aside. One blunt finger slowly traced the smaller circle of her nipple, and it swelled visibly, tightening under his touch. Caitlin felt that small, betraying movement all the way to her navel and lower, where moist heat flooded her.

"Your nipples are darker." He cupped his palm beneath the curve of her breast and cradled the silky weight. "And your breasts are fuller."

His fingers stroked compulsively over the silky skin. His eyes were heavy-lidded and sleepy, the blue irises shards of burning sapphire between tawny lashes. "I love your breasts," he said, his voice thick and unsteady. "I love the way they look, the way they feel, the way the nipples push against my palm when I stroke them. I lie awake nights dreaming about how you taste."

"Trey."

She said his name like a prayer, driven by the need that coiled in her belly, drummed in her veins and clawed at her heart.

Trey knew she was incapable of refusing him in that moment, and he held onto sanity by a thread. But she hadn't asked, and he'd made a promise. Much as he wanted to strip the jeans away from her legs and bury himself inside her, he knew that if he did, he'd lose her.

So instead of sucking her nipple into his mouth and feasting on her, he settled for taking her mouth with his, his fingers shaking in their effort to keep from crushing her and her too-sensitive breasts against him.

Caitlin welcomed the thrust of his tongue and the touch of his callused fingers against her heated skin. She wanted him so desperately that when he groaned and tore his mouth from hers, she murmured a frantic protest. But his fingers left her breast, and he wrapped her close against him, one hand cradling the back of her head to press her face against the base of his throat. His pulse raced wildly beneath her lips. Sanity slowly returned, but his pulse still beat too swiftly when he set her upright on his lap and fastened her bra and shirt with fingers that held a faint tremor.

''I wish I'd never promised you,'' he said, his voice rough in contrast to the gentle carefulness of his fingers. ''This no-sex rule of yours is going to drive us both crazy.'' He finished buttoning her jacket and smoothed the collar beneath her chin. His hot blue stare met hers. ''Making love with you has always been incredible. If pregnancy is making the rest of your body as sensitive as your breasts, just think how good sex would be.'' He lifted her off his lap and settled her onto the seat, easing the seat belt across her and latching it. ''Think about the two of us together, naked, with my mouth on your breasts.'' He bent closer, his nose almost touching hers. ''Tell me you want me, damn it.'' He breathed the last words against her lips before he dropped a swift, hard kiss against her mouth.

He slid across the seat, grabbed his hat from the dashboard, shoved open the door and stepped out.

Caitlin watched him unhook the gate and drag it open while she struggled to catch her breath. Trey was fiercely, possessively male, and Caitlin knew that giving him entry to her body meant ceding him the right to claim her as a mate. She was determined that he cede her equal rights to his heart before she agreed to marry him. Indulging in the need to kiss and touch was self-inflicted torture, but Caitlin could only hope that his physical desire for her would eventually lead to the lowering of the emotional walls behind which he'd barricaded his heart.

When they reached the Drummond ranch, they discovered that not only was Caitlin's grandmother still present, but Jennifer Hightower and CeCe Colby had obviously come to visit.

"Looks like the troops are here in force," Trey commented, switching off the truck engine and setting the brake.

"Yes, but having my aunts here draws my grandmother's attention away from me," Caitlin said with a smile. Hand on the door handle, she glanced at Trey. "You're coming in, aren't you?"

"I don't know if I should. I haven't seen Jennifer and CeCe since your pregnancy became public knowledge. Do you think it's safe for me to enter a house filled with your female friends and relatives?"

"Of course. What can they do—shoot you?" She

laughed at the swift roll of his eyes and pushed open her door to slide out.

Trey followed her into the house. The sound of feminine voices and laughter drew them down the hall to the kitchen, where they found the group of women seated around the table, drinking tea and chatting, while their daughters played nearby. They all greeted Caitlin and Trey with a chorus of hellos.

"And where have you two been this afternoon?" Sarah asked.

"Trey drove me to Uncle Wes's north pasture to visit the horses," Caitlin responded, accepting the chair and a cup of herbal tea offered by her aunt.

With easy familiarity, Trey took a mug from the cupboard, poured coffee and leaned his hips against the counter, his long legs crossed at the ankle. "We weren't the only ones checking out Caitlin's horses," he commented.

"Really? Who else was there?" Jennifer asked with interest.

"We don't know who exactly," Caitlin volunteered.

"She didn't stop to introduce herself," Trey added.

Their interest caught, the four women, together with Alexie, Samantha and Jessica, turned curious gazes to Caitlin.

"It was a little girl I've never seen before," Caitlin said. "When we reached the gate, there was a child sitting bareback on Christmas Girl. I thought it was a boy until she climbed through the fence and the barbed wire snagged her hat and pulled it off. Then a mane of carroty red hair tumbled to her shoulders.''

''Red hair?'' Jennifer asked.

''*Very* red,'' Caitlin confirmed. ''It's just a guess, but I think she might be about nine or ten years old, although she was too far away for me to be sure.''

''Hmm.'' CeCe glanced at Jessica. ''Who do we know who's maybe nine years old with red hair?''

''The only girl with red hair that I know is Analisa Watkins,'' Jessica responded. ''But she lives in Butte Creek. I don't know what she'd be doing way out in Uncle Wes's pasture.''

''Jessica's right.'' Samantha's voice chimed in. ''The only girl in school with red hair is Analisa.''

''Missy Turlow told me that Analisa's mother is dating the new man that Uncle Wes hired a few months ago,'' CeCe offered. ''Perhaps Analisa is visiting at the ranch with her mother.''

''But we didn't see any other riders, and the child was apparently alone. Surely her mother wouldn't have let her ride off by herself?'' Caitlin glanced around the table and found the women shaking their heads with varying degrees of dismay.

''Lucinda Watkins is a marginal parent, at best,'' Patricia Drummond said briskly, her no-nonsense tone conveying disapproval. ''She's a barmaid on the late shift at the Longneck Saloon, and I understand she often leaves the little girl alone while she's at work.''

''Her mom doesn't get up in the morning and make Analisa breakfast,'' Alexie added, her eyes solemn.

"And Analisa doesn't have any pretty clothes. Her mom makes her wear old jeans and T-shirts."

Caitlin flinched. The picture her family painted of Analisa Watkins's life was all too familiar. A careless mother too focused on her boyfriends; a daughter struggling to survive and parent herself. Cold meals eaten alone in a house with a mother gone to work or out to a party. Trying to be quiet when her mother was sleeping in with her current boyfriend or exhausted from a late night out. Caitlin knew exactly what life was like for a child, for it was a description of her own life until she was twelve and her mother's current boyfriend gave her a black eye. She'd packed her knapsack, hitched from Los Angeles to Montana and asked her aunt Sarah for sanctuary. Caitlin knew in vivid, painful detail how terrifying a child's life could be.

Not for my baby, she vowed. *My child will be loved and cared for. I'll never miss a chance to tell him or her how much I love them. And I'll never leave them alone, lonely and afraid.*

"Some people shouldn't be allowed to have children," Sarah said tightly.

"No," Caitlin agreed. She reached out and gently squeezed her aunt's hand where it lay atop the table. "But fortunately, sometimes people like you rescue children with absent mothers."

Sarah's expression softened, and she smiled, turning her hand over to return Caitlin's affectionate squeeze. "Thanks, sweetie." She glanced at the clock above the refrigerator and gasped. ''My goodness, look at the time! And I haven't started dinner yet.''

Jennifer and CeCe echoed her surprise and stood. The kitchen bustled with activity as the women gathered coats and children and left for their own kitchens and hungry families.

''Time for me to go, too.'' Trey rinsed his mug at the sink and turned it upside down on the drainboard to dry.

''Can't you stay for dinner?'' Sarah asked.

''I have chores to do,'' he answered. ''But I'll take a rain check—how about tomorrow night?'' He asked Sarah, but he looked at Caitlin, a question in the lift of his brow. She nodded and he relaxed.

''You're welcome any night, Trey,'' Sarah answered.

''Thanks.'' He pushed away from the counter and held out a hand to Caitlin. ''Walk me out, Caitlin?''

She put her hand in his and let him tug her upright. He shifted his hand to the small of her back as they left the kitchen and walked down the hall. The light touch sent a surge of anticipation through her veins to curl in the pit of her stomach.

Trey paused at the front door and turned her to face him.

''When do you want to move the horses?''

''I'm not sure. I need to talk to Wes.''

''The sooner they're moved, the better. We could get snow any day.''

''I know,'' she agreed.

"Let me know when you've talked to Wes. I'll get some men together."

"And some women," Caitlin reminded him. "If we don't let my aunts and Samantha, Alexie and Jessica join us, we'll never hear the end of it."

"True." Trey's mouth lifted in a smile of wry acceptance before it faded and his gaze sharpened. "You're not riding, are you?"

"No," Caitlin reassured him. "But I'll be there—probably driving Uncle Josh's work truck."

Trey breathed a sigh of relief. "You can drive my pickup," he said. "That old truck of Josh's hasn't had a decent set of springs since 1952."

"Hmm." Caitlin narrowed her eyes consideringly. "You're actually offering to let another human being drive your precious truck?"

He reddened under her teasing. "Yeah, well, only if you promise not to dent it. And I let other people drive my truck," he added defensively.

"What?" Caitlin clapped a hand to her heart in pretend shock. "When did this miracle occur? And why didn't I get a news bulletin about it?"

His eyes glinted, and a reluctant smile tilted the corner of his mouth. "Did anyone ever tell you that you have a smart mouth?" he asked with amusement.

"Yes," she answered promptly, laughing at him. "You did—often, if I remember correctly."

"Hmm." He brushed his fingertips along the curve of her bottom lip before trailing them over her cheek. "You're right. That was me, wasn't it? And it's still true."

For one perfect moment, all barriers were gone, and Caitlin basked in the warmth of the easy affection she'd taken for granted when she was a child. Then Trey's expression became shuttered, and his fingers left her cheek. He pulled open the door and stepped over the threshold.

"I'll talk to Lucas and Josh and a few others. Let me know if you have a chance to talk to Wes tonight."

"I'll call you if I catch him at home."

"Right. See you tomorrow."

He touched his forefinger to the brim of his hat in goodbye and loped down the steps.

Caitlin had expected him to kiss her goodbye, but he strode down the walk to his truck and slid behind the wheel without a backward glance. Dust rose beneath the pickup's wheels as he drove away. A cold gust of wind sent a dried leaf skittering across the porch floor, and Caitlin shivered, hugging herself for warmth as she stepped inside the house and closed the door.

It's probably just as well he didn't kiss me, she reflected.

Four days passed before Caitlin's horses were moved. The moment word got out that the herd of horses was going to be driven cross-country to the Hildebrandt headquarters, she was besieged by pleas from her younger cousins to participate. Caitlin decided to postpone the drive until the weekend to accommodate the excited youngsters. Fortunately, Saturday dawned bright and clear.

Pickup trucks with horse trailers crowded the open space between barn and house where the good-natured Wes gradually sorted out horses and riders and organized them into a loose group. Trey, Wes, Lucas, Josh, Wayne, J.J., Zach Colby, Murphy Redman and Charlie Allen were joined by Jennifer, Sarah, CeCe, and all six of the younger Hightower and Colby kids. All the riders were bundled into warm jackets, mufflers and gloves against the chill wind that swept down off the buttes to ruffle their horses' manes and tails and set the vanes on the old windmill beyond the barn whirling.

Shielded from the brisk wind that reddened the riders' cheeks, Caitlin sat behind the steering wheel of Trey's truck, her arm propped on the open window, the heater warming her toes. Trey left the semicircle of riders where Wes gave last-minute instructions and reined his gelding next to Caitlin. The gelding nuzzled her jacket sleeve, and she stroked the baby-soft underside of his muzzle.

"Hello, there," she crooned. The horse's eyes half closed with pleasure at her petting, and he stretched his neck to move closer. "What a sweetheart you are, Jiggs," she exclaimed softly, smoothing her hand down the blaze that ran from forehead to nostrils. She glanced at Trey.

"Aren't you worried about riding him today?"

"No."

"But the pasture's rough, and who knows how

many hidden holes there may be. CeCe told me that you bought Jiggs for team roping. What if he steps in a hole?''

''We'll be careful.'' Trey stroked a gloved hand down the quarter horse's satiny shoulder, ending with an affectionate pat. ''Besides, it wouldn't matter how much I paid for him, I still wouldn't want him to step in a hole and break a leg.''

''I know. I'm just concerned.''

''About Jiggs? Aren't you worried about *me* breaking my neck if he steps in a hole and goes down?''

''Of course. If you break your neck, who will get my horses home?''

''You're a coldhearted woman, Caitlin Drummond.'' He shook his head in disbelief, his eyes glinting with laughter.

''Cold is the operative word here, Weber.'' She glanced out the windshield at the riders. ''I'm the only one who has a chance of staying warm today.''

Trey looked past her at the horses and riders. ''I wouldn't be surprised if you had a few kids piling into the cab with you before this is over.'' He glanced at the horizon, where gray clouds threatened. ''The weatherman didn't predict snow, but it's still cold.''

His gaze returned to Caitlin. She'd tugged a knit cap over her ears, and wisps of black hair escaped the red wool to curl around her face and nape where her coat collar was turned up against the cold. He wondered briefly if their child would have her black hair and green eyes or his blond hair and blue eyes.

''Have you talked to J.J.?''

"No," he answered absentmindedly, still distracted by the mental image of a chubby-cheeked baby with black curls and green eyes.

"He might be a little—" Caitlin searched for the right word "—difficult," she added diplomatically.

"Difficult?" He crossed his forearms atop the saddle horn and gave her his full attention. "What's wrong?"

"He's not happy that I'm pregnant—and he blames you. I told him that I don't need a knight to defend me, nor an adopted brother to hold a shotgun on my baby's father, but he's not convinced."

"I'll deal with him," Trey said.

Caitlin eyed him with some trepidation. "I think he wants to punch you, Trey," she added with concern.

"I'm sure he's not the only member of your family who feels that way," he said grimly. "I said I'll deal with him."

"I don't want you and J.J. to fight over me, Trey."

"Marry me, and he won't have any reason to fight me."

"He doesn't have any reason to fight you now," she said firmly. "I'm not a teenager who's been taken advantage of. I'm a grown woman, and I can deal with my own life."

"Whether you can deal with your life or not doesn't change the way the men in your family feel about you being pregnant and unmarried," Trey said grimly. "And that includes me."

She met his narrowed stare with a calm, level gaze. ''Are we going to fight about this today?''

''No.'' He bit the word out. ''We're not going to fight about it. I told you I accept that you need time to make up your mind, but that doesn't mean that I've changed my mind about our getting married soon.''

''All right,'' she said mildly. ''As long as we understand each other. And I'd really prefer that you not do battle with J.J. over this. I don't want him to have a black eye or loose teeth because of me.''

Trey stared at her for a moment before his face softened with amusement. ''What makes you think that *I* won't be the one who loses teeth? J.J.'s sixteen years younger than me, and he works out by lifting weights.''

Caitlin eyed Trey. Even dressed in the ordinary rancher's work clothes of boots, worn Levi's, faded jean jacket, gloves and hat, he still looked dangerous. Caitlin wondered briefly, and not for the first time, just exactly what kinds of assignments he'd faced during the years he'd spent in the military. He rarely talked about what he'd done or where he'd been, but the scars on his body testified to the hazards of his work. She shook her head slowly. ''You look like you could lick your weight in wildcats. I doubt my cousin would have a chance, so please be diplomatic.''

''Diplomatic.'' He shook his head in resignation. ''I'll try. But you have to promise to bandage my cuts and bruises when he's done with me.''

''Hmm.'' Caitlin pretended to consider refusing

him before she nodded. ''All right, but if you bleed all over me, you have to pay the cleaning bill.''

Trey laughed. ''Like I said, you're a coldhearted woman, Caitlin Drummond.''

He leaned forward and gave her a quick, hard kiss before he straightened and reined the quarter horse away from the truck. ''One of us will open the gates. You stay in the truck where it's warm,'' he instructed.

''Is that an order?'' She frowned, eyes narrowing.

''No, ma'am,'' he said solemnly. ''That's a request. Please.''

''All right. Since you asked so nicely, you can open gates for me.''

''And you can owe me. I'll collect later.''

He lifted Jiggs into a fast walk and joined Wes at the head of the riders as they left the ranchyard.

Caitlin shifted the truck into gear and followed them, her blood beating faster after his quick kiss and promise of more later.

Trey and Wes's crew of riders, trailed by Caitlin in the pickup, passed through the last gate into the north pasture and gathered in a circle around the truck for instructions.

''This isn't going to be easy,'' Wes warned the kids, his deep voice whiskey-rough. ''This pasture is home to these horses, and they aren't going to be too anxious to leave it.'' He gestured at the men in the group. ''We've made this drive a good many times over the years and learned that the best way to get it done is to bunch the herd and run them down the fence line to the gates. All the gates between here and home are located in the corners of the pastures, and we left all of them wide open. If we're lucky, we'll be able to bunch the horses and keep the fences on one side of them and us on the other. We'll run them along the fence lines and funnel the herd through the gates into the next pasture.'' He glanced around the group. ''Everybody understand? Any questions? No? All right, then. Josh, you and Zach take a few folks with you and post them on the far side of the gate. J.J., you and Wayne take three or four riders, fan out on this side in case they try to break away from the gate. Caitlin, you post that truck at the end of the line. Trey, Lucas and the rest of us will round up the herd and get them movin' toward you all.''

''Sounds easy, doesn't it?''

Caitlin glanced away from Wes. Josh sat easily on a chestnut gelding, horse and rider near enough to touch. ''Isn't it?'' she asked. ''It seems simple.''

''Somebody ought to explain that to those mule-headed horses of yours,'' he commented, grinning at her. ''The minute we start easing them toward that first gate, they usually decide they don't want to go. From then on, it's a free-for-all.''

''Is it dangerous?'' Disconcerted, Caitlin's gaze flicked to her little cousins, her aunts and then to Trey. He and Wes, with several other riders, were just disappearing over the rise beyond the stock tank.

''Nah—not unless one of the horses steps in a hole and goes down. Mostly, it's just frustrating if the herd decides to be stubborn.'' He leaned sideways in the saddle and tugged a silky black curl that lay against her cheek. "Don't worry. I wouldn't have let the kids come along if I thought there was any serious danger. You better move the truck into line. If Wes comes charging over that hill with the horses and you're still sitting here, you'll be in serious trouble."

He moved off, and Caitlin followed Wes's instructions, easing the truck forward over the hillocks and hollows to take her assigned place.

Long moments went by while she waited. Ten minutes. Twenty.

Caitlin glanced at her watch for the second time in as many minutes.

"A half hour," she murmured aloud. She leaned out her window and scanned the far slope where the fence disappeared over the crest of the rise. Nothing moved. Disappointed, she sighed and started the truck's engine to warm the cab's slowly chilling interior.

Another ten minutes went by. Caitlin fiddled with the radio, humming softly along with a country ballad.

"I hear something."

Caitlin snapped to attention at J.J.'s shout and sat forward expectantly, gripping the steering wheel, her gaze once again searching the fence line. She heard nothing, saw nothing but the brown autumn grass and empty skyline.

Then a rumble like growing thunder reached her ears over the low growl of the truck engine.

"They're coming," she whispered.

She'd seen horses and cattle moved hundreds of

times, but the sight of riders and animals in motion never failed to leave her awed.

One moment the skyline was bare, the next moment it was alive with moving color. The horses crested the hill and spilled down the slope in a flood of moving brown, black and red. Their heads high, their manes and tails streaming in bright banners against the gray sky, their hoofbeats shook the ground and rolled like thunder. Riders whistled and yelled, racing alongside and behind the herd.

In moments, they were past Caitlin. J.J., Wayne and the riders posted between Caitlin and the next gate spurred their horses, joining Trey and his group as they crowded the herd, funneling them through the fence into the next pasture. She shifted the truck into gear and followed them, stopping just beyond the opening to jump out and close the gate behind her, preventing the herd from returning to their home pasture.

"So far, so good," she murmured as she climbed into the truck. But she knew the easy part was over. There were three more pastures and gates to go through before reaching home, and there weren't riders posted before and after those gates. Ahead of her, the horses were still bunched together, but the herd wasn't as compact as it had been. Even as she watched, a young gelding broke away, eluded the drovers and raced off across the pasture. The riders managed to frustrate the two mares that tried to follow the gelding, forcing them into the moving herd. "So much for the easy part." Caitlin sighed. Steering with one hand, she jotted a brief note about the gelding on the clipboard resting on the seat beside her and pulled through the next gate. She stopped the truck and closed the gate, hurrying to return to the pickup and move on, anxious to keep the herd and riders in sight.

By the time the herd reached the pasture beyond Wes's barns and Caitlin closed the last gate, another five horses had joined the gelding in his successful bid for freedom. She parked the pickup next to the corral and joined Wes and her cousins on the top rail.

''Well, missy, they're home for the winter,'' Wes commented, his weathered face creasing in a smile. His eyes gleamed with a youthful enthusiasm that belied his white hair. ''Hell of a lot of fun, wasn't it?''

Caitlin laughed and slipped an arm around his shoulders in a quick hug. ''Yes, it was. I can't wait until next year when I can ride instead of drive.''

''Yes, but at least the truck has a heater and you got to stay warm!'' Alexie shivered. Her cheeks were red with cold, her eyes bright with the excitement of the drive. ''I'm going inside to thaw out my fingers and toes. Aunt Molly said she'd have hot chocolate and lunch for us when we got back, and I'm starving.''

''Me, too,'' Samantha put in. She clambered to the ground and looked at her mother, still perched with the others atop the corral rail. ''Are you coming in, Mom?''

''Yes, I could use something hot to drink.'' Sarah swung her leg over the rail and descended.

"Me, too," Jennifer and CeCe chorused. They joined Sarah on the ground and paused.

"Are you coming, Caitlin?"

"In a minute," she said absently, busy searching the milling horses for any signs of injury. Behind her, she heard the fading chatter of women, girls and boys as they walked toward the house.

"How many did we lose?"

She looked over her shoulder. Trey swung down from Jiggs and looped the reins over a lower corral rail before he climbed easily and sat beside her.

"Only six."

"That's not bad," he commented.

"Not bad?" Wes snorted. "Hell, it's a bloody miracle, that's what it is. Two years ago we spent six hours and only got half of them home. Spent the next four days collecting the rest of them and then we had to lure them with grain."

Trey grinned. "Let me guess—I'll bet the last one to come in was that black mare with the white socks."

"Yup." Wes nodded abruptly. "How'd you know that, boy?"

"Because she gave us the most trouble today," Trey replied. He glanced at Caitlin. "There must be something about black-haired females," he drawled. "They're just plain difficult."

"Hmph." Caitlin refused to be drawn in. She cast one more sweeping glance over the herd, reassuring herself that they'd come to no harm. "I'm going to get something hot to drink. How about you guys?"

"I think I'll join you," Wes said. "These old bones of mine seem to get stiffer the colder I get." He eased himself carefully down the rails and waited as Caitlin did the same.

"Are you coming, Trey?" Caitlin looked at him.

"In a minute. I have to rub Jiggs down and give him some grain. He's earned it. And I have one more thing to settle." His gaze lifted to look beyond her.

Caitlin glanced over her shoulder. J.J. leaned against a corral pole several yards away. He wasn't even pretending to watch the horses. His green eyes were narrowed over Caitlin and Trey, his face stony.

"Trey, I—"

"Don't worry, Caitlin." Trey cupped her chin in his gloved palm and turned her face to his. "It'll be fine."

"No black eyes," she said softly.

"Not for him." Trey smiled fleetingly. "I can't promise whether he'll give me one or not."

She hesitated, but Trey smoothed his thumb over her cheek in a brief caress before he dropped his hand to his thigh. "Go inside where it's warm."

Wes pulled Caitlin's arm through his and urged her toward the house.

"Don't worry, missy. Those two had to butt heads sooner or later. Might as well be sooner."

Trey's gaze followed Caitlin's slim form until she climbed the porch steps and entered the house, leaving him and J.J. alone outside. Then he dropped to the ground and unlooped Jiggs's reins from the rail before he turned to face a potential enemy.

Chapter Six

"I want to talk to you." The words were hard-edged, J.J.'s face grim.

"All right," Trey said evenly. He glanced at the house, then at J.J. "Let's go into the barn."

Trey led the way, Jiggs plodding behind him, his muzzle bumping gently against Trey's shoulder. He slid the heavy doors wide and walked the horse into the barn, passing the stalls occupied with the other riders' horses, contentedly munching hay and grain. He stopped in front of an empty stall and ground hitched Jiggs. Beside him, J.J. did the same with his horse. Trey hooked the stirrup over the saddle horn and loosened the girth, then pulled the saddle and blanket from Jiggs's back and swung them over the top board of the stall.

J.J. did the same with his horse, the two men working silently to rub down the horses and settle them into their separate stalls. Both horses were feeding on hay and grain when Trey stepped into the aisle and latched the gate behind him. Then he turned to face J.J.

"You wanted to talk to me?"

"My mother told me that Caitlin's pregnant and you're the father."

"That's true."

J.J.'s green eyes turned to ice, and a muscle flexed in his jaw.

"When I asked Caitlin what you're going to do about the baby, she told me that she's not sure if you're going to marry her."

Trey tensed. "She said that? In those exact words?"

"Close enough," J.J. said ominously, his hands closing into fists. "Now you tell me why you won't marry her."

"I'd marry her in a heartbeat." Trey shot the words back. "Today, if she'd have me."

Confusion flickered swiftly across J.J.'s features. "Then why did she say she wasn't sure if the two of you are getting married?"

"Because she's not sure *she* wants to marry *me.*"

"She's not sure...." J.J. shook his head in disbelief, his fists loosening as he planted his hands on his hips and stared at Trey. "What the hell kind of sense does that make?" he demanded bluntly. "You mean to tell me that *she's* the one who doesn't want to get married?''

''I didn't say she doesn't want to get married,'' Trey corrected him. ''I said she's not sure.''

J.J. stared at him for a long moment before he yanked off his Stetson and plowed the fingers of one hand through his blond hair. ''So exactly what's going on here?''

''She wants time to be sure that marriage is right for her, and I've agreed to give her all the time she needs.''

''But you're sure that *you* want to get married?''

''Oh, yeah,'' Trey said. ''I want to get married.'' His tone left no doubt that he meant the words.

''Why don't you just tell her that this is your baby, too, and you're getting married?''

''I tried that,'' Trey said. ''She wasn't convinced.''

A wry grin slowly eased the taut lines of J.J.'s face. ''That sounds like our Caitlin.'' He lifted an eyebrow and eyed Trey consideringly. ''Why don't you just tie her up, throw her in the truck and haul her off to a preacher?''

Trey sighed, the sound a near groan. ''God knows I've considered it. But I don't want to start our marriage with my wife furious with me because I'm the one who held the shotgun and forced her to marry me. Besides,'' he added, ''I understand that pregnant women can be a little emotional. I'm trying to be considerate while I'm waiting for her to come to her senses.''

''Women,'' J.J. said with empathy. ''You know,''

he commented, "I was ready to break your nose and maybe a few ribs for not doing right by my cousin. Apparently, I should have been having this talk with her, instead."

"No, don't do that. I'll take care of it," Trey said quickly, determined that Caitlin remain free of pressure. He started to walk slowly down the aisle toward the big outer doors, and J.J. fell into step next to him. "Besides," he added with an amused grin. "What made you think you could take me, kid?"

"Kid?" J.J. laughed. "I've been working out, old man, while you've been sitting around the house getting soft."

"Yeah, right." Trey scoffed.

They reached the porch's bottom step, and J.J. stopped Trey with a hand on his arm. Trey halted and looked at the younger man. J.J.'s green eyes were serious, all levity gone.

"She deserves to be happy, Trey. Whatever it is that makes her unsure about marrying you, fix it."

Trey couldn't tell him that he'd give his right arm to be able to fix what was keeping Caitlin undecided. "I'll try, J.J.—I am trying."

J.J. nodded curtly, and dropped his hand from Trey's arm. "Guess I can't ask more than that."

He mounted the steps, and Trey followed him, both men entering a house that was filled with children, adults, dogs and the occasional cat. The chaos was warmly welcoming. Trey shed his coat and hat, and driven by a need he couldn't explain, he moved through the rooms until he found Caitlin in the crowded kitchen. She leaned against the counter near the coffeemaker, a gently steaming mug cradled in her hands.

He crossed the room and joined her, bracing his hand behind her on the countertop and nudging her hip with his. She glanced up and smiled. He couldn't smile back. J.J.'s words had set loose a maelstrom of emotions. He wanted her to marry him. He wanted to have the right to take her home with him, to sleep with her each night and wake with her curled against him, sleepy and warm, every morning. Most of all, he wanted to erase whatever doubts she had about him that kept her from coming freely to him.

He wanted to make her happy. Whatever it took.

Caitlin's smile faded, the welcome in her eyes changing to inquiry, and Trey realized that he'd been staring at her. He didn't know for how long.

''Hi.'' He managed to get one word out.

''Hi.'' Her gaze searched his, a tiny frown drawing her brows into a faint vee. ''I don't see any bruises, and J.J. was laughing when he came in, so your talk must have gone well. Is there something else wrong, Trey?''

''No. Nothing's wrong.'' He glanced at the cup she held. ''Is that hot?''

''Yes, but...''

He took the mug from her and lifted it to his lips for a sip. It wasn't coffee, and he grimaced, then bent close to whisper, ''What the hell is this?''

''Herbal tea—chamomile, actually.'' She laughed.

His expression told her that he thought the tea was revolting. "It's good for you."

"Thanks, but I think I'll stick with coffee." He glanced up and realized that everyone in the room was watching him and Caitlin with varying expressions—curiosity, interest, amusement and speculation. Even Alexie and Samantha were looking at them with starry-eyed romanticism. He frowned, and his gaze swept the room. "What?" he demanded, irritated.

Josh grinned, shrugged and exchanged glances with Sarah while the rest of the relatives and friends crowding the big kitchen only laughed and resumed their conversations.

Four days later, Trey walked out of the feed store, shifted a sack of grain off his shoulder and dropped it into the bed of his pickup on top of the other six bags. He slammed the tailgate closed and brushed grain dust off the shoulder of his jacket before he started across the street toward the cafe. Halfway across the pavement, he saw Caitlin entering the grocery store, so he changed direction to follow her.

He caught up with her in the produce section. "Afternoon, sweetheart."

Caitlin spun quickly, a delighted smile spreading across her face. "Trey! What are you doing here?"

"Following you." He smiled at her, struck anew by the healthy glow of her skin, the sheen of her ebony hair and the brightness of her emerald eyes. "What are you doing here? I thought you went grocery shopping yesterday—or did you tell me that just to get out of helping Josh and me comb the pasture for that black gelding of yours?''

''No, honest.'' She sketched a quick X over her heart. ''I did, but I had to make a quick trip today to pick up a few things for a celebration dinner tonight.''

''What's the occasion?''

''Samantha got an A plus on a big math test. And, believe me, that rates a major celebration. She worked her little heart out studying for it, and all of us drilled her, so we all had a hand in her success.''

''Uh-oh, does that mean you won't consider going out to dinner with me tonight?''

''I can't, Trey.'' Regret tinged her words. ''This really is a big event. Samantha struggles with math, and we want to be as supportive as possible.'' She brightened. ''But why don't you have dinner with us?''

Trey loved Caitlin's family, but he hadn't had her to himself for nearly a week, and he was feeling starved. He was also beginning to suspect that Caitlin was purposely avoiding being alone with him. ''What time are you eating?''

''Probably around five.''

''Then we'll have plenty of time after dinner to go out somewhere.'' His gaze held Caitlin's. ''A movie, maybe?''

''Maybe,'' she agreed, not promising. Caitlin was cautious about spending time alone with Trey. She knew very well that he wouldn't cross the physical boundaries she'd set, but she wasn't convinced of her ability to stand firm.

Her attention was diverted by a child who stood at the end of the next aisle, back turned to them. Something about the ragged little figure seemed naggingly familiar, but it wasn't until the child turned slightly, revealing a curl of carroty hair tucked behind one ear, that Caitlin realized where she'd seen the girl before.

"Trey," she whispered urgently, catching his forearm. "Isn't that the little girl we saw on top of my mare in the north pasture?"

Trey glanced over his shoulder to focus thoughtfully on the slight figure. "Could be," he agreed.

The child was clearly unaware that she was being watched. She glanced furtively around, then quickly snatched a bag of cookies off the shelf and stuffed it inside her jacket.

"She's stealing food," Caitlin gasped softly. "She's much too thin. And why isn't she in school?"

"Good question," Trey muttered, frowning as he registered the condition of her jeans and T-shirt. "She looks like she slept in her clothes."

Caitlin recognized the signs of a neglected child all too well. Looking at the worn jacket and jeans smudged with dirt, the tangled mop of hair and the too-thin body was like looking at herself at that age.

"She looks like a child without a mother."

The girl disappeared around the corner of the aisle. Caitlin and Trey exchanged quick glances and followed, pausing to peer down the aisle after her. She stood a few feet away in front of a shelved display of canned soup. Her jacket pockets bulged suspiciously. She glanced over her shoulder, and the two adults quickly moved back, barely escaping being seen.

"She's definitely shoplifting food," Caitlin whispered.

"We've got two choices," Trey commented. "Let the store clerk catch her and call the sheriff, or catch her ourselves, empty her pockets and take her over to the cafe for a hamburger."

"What a good idea!" Caitlin beamed with relief. "Let's go get her."

She started forward, but Trey stopped her with a hand on her forearm.

"Not so fast. I doubt that we can just walk up to her—especially when she's got her pockets full of stolen food. She's probably going to run." He glanced around the corner, his gaze sweeping the empty aisle. "She's gone. I'll go to the far end of this aisle. You walk toward the back of the store at this end. If you see her, move toward her as casually as possible, and we'll try to pin her between us. Okay?"

Caitlin nodded, and Trey strode quickly down the aisle and disappeared around the corner. Caitlin began walking, glancing down the aisles as she went. Three aisles down, Caitlin spotted her.

Trey had already turned the corner and was strolling toward her. The girl glanced up, her deep brown eyes suspicious. While she was looking at Caitlin, Trey reached her.

''Mornin',' he drawled. The little girl spun quickly, her eyes filled with fear.

''Mornin',' she mumbled.

She stepped to one side to go around him. Trey closed his hand over her shoulder.

''Hold on a minute,'' he said gently, firmly.

The girl panicked. Small fists shoved at his hand, and the hard toe of her tennis shoe connected with his shin.

Trey bit off an oath and frowned at the little girl. ''Stop that,'' he ordered. ''And stop squirming. I'm not going to hurt you.''

She responded by twisting her head and biting his hand.

''Ouch!'' Trey grabbed the waistband of her jeans at the small of her back and shifted his hand from her shoulder to her coat collar. ''Now hold still,'' he commanded, his deep voice carrying a warning.

She twisted and looked at him, fury mingled with fear in her eyes. ''Let me go,'' she said fiercely, her voice just above a whisper.

''We aren't going to hurt you,'' Caitlin told her, her voice purposely soothing and gentle. ''We're on our way to the cafe to have lunch, and we thought you might want to go with us.''

The girl stilled, but the gaze that met Caitlin's was no less hostile and wary.

''You don't even know me, why'd you want to feed me?''

''No reason.'' Caitlin told the small white lie without a qualm. ''We just thought you might like to join us.''

''And tell us where you learned to ride Christmas Girl without a saddle and bridle,'' Trey added dryly. The girl looked over her shoulder at him, her expression blank. ''Out at Wes Hildebrandt's north pasture? The quarter horse mare you were riding when we drove up and you took off?'' Trey elaborated.

The girl's thin body stiffened, and she blanched. Her gaze flicked from Trey to Caitlin. ''I didn't hurt the horse,'' she said quickly. ''I was just sitting on her till you showed up and then I rode her to the fence and let her go.''

''I know Christmas Girl wasn't hurt,'' Caitlin said gently.

Analisa was defensive, fearful, and much too quick to assume that she would be punished. Caitlin recognized the knee-jerk response to adult interest all too well. Long before she reached Analisa's age, she'd become adept at avoiding her mother and the male friends that flitted through their life. She hadn't known what safety was until she'd run away from her mother's home in L.A. and hitched to Montana to live with Sarah and Josh. *Not my baby,* she vowed again. *My baby won't learn to fear adults. Trey and I will keep him safe.*

''We're curious about where you learned to ride like that,'' Trey added. ''Maybe you're a jockey?''

Confused, the girl frowned at him. ''No, I'm not a jockey. I just like to ride horses. I don't have one of my own, but sometimes my mom's friends let me ride one of theirs while they're visiting with my mom.''

''Ah.'' Caitlin glanced pointedly up and down the aisle, empty but for the three of them. ''Where is your mom?''

''She's at work.'' The response was swift, flat.

Caitlin didn't fail to notice that the child's body tensed, and she refused to meet Caitlin's gaze.

''Well, then.'' She smiled encouragingly. ''I'm sure she won't mind if you have a sandwich with us.''

Fear vied with hunger in the child's gaze until hunger won out. ''I guess not,'' she said reluctantly, carefully.

''Good. Come on, we're all starving and you can tell us more stories about learning to ride.'' Caitlin caught one of the girl's fists in her hand, ignoring the fact that the little fingers refused to uncurl. She glanced at Trey, and he released his hold on the back of the child's jeans and jacket. ''I'm Caitlin Drummond. The guy behind you is Trey Weber. What's your name?''

''Analisa.'' The child stood perfectly still, her fist enclosed in Caitlin's hand, her wary gaze searching Caitlin's. ''Analisa Watkins. Aren't you Samantha's cousin?''

''Yes, I am.'' Caitlin smiled warmly at the little girl. ''You must go to school with Samantha, don't you?''

''Yeah.'' The thin shoulders lost some of their rigidity. ''But she's bigger than I am. We're not in the same grade.'' She looked at Caitlin. ''I guess it's okay if I go to the cafe with you. I'm not supposed to talk to strangers, but I know Samantha, so I guess her cousin's not a stranger."

"No, definitely not." Caitlin nodded solemnly, breathing a silent sigh of relief when Analisa's fingers uncurled. But then the little girl tugged slightly in a demand for release. For one brief moment, Caitlin considered clutching her tighter but then freed her hand. *If she runs away, we'll find her. I'm sure the school district has an address for her and her mother.*

But Analisa didn't run. She tucked her hands into her jacket pockets.

Caitlin knew immediately that Analisa had forgotten the soup cans that crowded her pockets. The little girl's eyes widened in consternation, her gaze flying to meet Caitlin's. Thinking swiftly, Caitlin smiled reassuringly.

"We need to find candles for a celebration cake. Do you happen to know what aisle they're in, Analisa?"

"Um, I think they're by the cake mixes." Analisa's face brightened. "That's closer to the front of the store."

"Oh, great." Caitlin caught Trey's arm and turned him with her toward the end of the aisle. "We'll just make a quick stop, then, and be on our way. Goodness," she said, ignoring the crackle of paper and the soft thunk and scrape of cans being hurriedly shoved onto a shelf behind them. "I'm just starving, aren't you, Trey?"

"I could eat a sandwich," he agreed.

The soft noises behind them ceased, and the adults halted, half-turning to look at the child.

"Are you coming, Analisa?" Caitlin asked.

"Yes."

Analisa followed them as they located the candles, paused at the checkstand to pay for their purchases, and then left the store for the cafe.

A short while later, seated in a wide booth at Connie's Cafe, Trey and Caitlin watched with amazement as Analisa ate a large cheeseburger with French fries, downed a strawberry milk shake and then eyed the waitress hopefully as she passed with dessert plates for customers in the booth behind them.

"I think I'll have chocolate cake for dessert," Trey commented. "Anybody else? How about you, Analisa?"

"Yes!" she answered promptly.

The little girl steadily worked her way through two pieces of chocolate cake—her own and the slice that Caitlin ordered but never intended to eat.

"Where did you say your mother went, Analisa?" Caitlin asked casually.

"She's on vacation with Gus," Analisa mumbled, her attention on balancing her fork with its bite of cake and fudge frosting.

The words were out before she remembered to be cautious. She froze, her eyes rounding in dismay.

Caitlin struggled to keep her expression neutral. Trey swallowed a mouthful of coffee and took another bite of cake, while Caitlin smiled at Analisa and gestured at the little girl's nearly empty plate.

"How's the cake?" she asked.

"Uh." Analisa looked blankly at her plate and back at Caitlin. "Good. Really good."

"Hmm, maybe I'll have some, after all."

"You can have the rest of mine," Trey offered. They exchanged a swift message of agreement before he slid the plate in front of her.

"Thank you. You know, Analisa," Caitlin said thoughtfully as she carefully cut a bite of cake. "I think you should come stay with me at Sarah's house until your mom comes home."

"Oh, no." Analisa refused quickly. "I can't. My mother said I wasn't to—"

"I know. You're not supposed to talk to strangers," Caitlin said when Analisa faltered. "But you know Samantha, which means her mom, Sarah, isn't a stranger, and I'm Samantha's cousin, and Trey is Samantha's good friend, so that means none of us are strangers, right?"

"I don't know." Analisa remained unconvinced. "I think my mom will be mad if she comes home and I'm not there."

"We can leave her a note. Then as soon as she comes home, she'll know where you are. And she'll probably be very glad that you were with Samantha while she was gone, because Sarah is a great cook and you'll have a lot of fun at her house."

"I don't think so."

The weary, much too-adult cynicism that colored Analisa's words nearly broke Caitlin's heart and made her so angry at the absentee mother that she could have cursed.

''Well, I think it's a wonderful idea,'' she said firmly. ''Samantha will be delighted to have the company, and we've plenty of room.''

Analisa looked doubtfully at Caitlin. ''Are you sure?''

''Absolutely,'' she said with a sharp nod.

Big brown eyes searched the adult faces before wariness gradually gave way to cautious optimism. ''Maybe it would be okay,'' she said slowly. ''But I hafta' go home the minute my mom gets back, or she'll be really mad at me. She says I gotta' stay in the house when she's gone or the neighbors will complain and I'll be in trouble with the police. I won't get in trouble with the police for staying at your house instead of mine, will I?''

''No, sweetie.'' Caitlin gave serious thought to murdering Analisa's mother. ''You won't get in trouble with the police. In fact, they'll be glad that you're with us. But just to be sure, we'll let them know where you are, okay?''

Analisa's face cleared, and the smile that curved her mouth lit her face. ''Okay.''

''Okay. That's settled.'' Caitlin glanced at the empty plates strewn across the table and the half-eaten slice of cake in front of Analisa. ''Why don't you finish your cake. Then we'll run by your house and pick up some clothes for you. We'll write a note for your mom, too, and tack it on the door so we're sure she'll find it as soon as she gets home.''

Analisa nodded and tucked the almost forgotten forkful of cake into her mouth.

''I'll follow you,'' Trey told Caitlin quietly as he walked beside her to her car after departing the cafe. ''Even if her mother's there, I'll be damned if I'll leave that kid with a woman who left her alone.''

''All right,'' Caitlin agreed softly so that Analisa couldn't hear from where she walked several steps ahead of them. ''And I'll call the police as soon as I can when we get home.''

''Good.'' He glanced at the little girl, but she clearly was paying no attention to their conversation. ''I hope they take her away and put her in a good home. There's no excuse for a mother to be so careless and irresponsible.''

''I agree,'' Caitlin said forcefully. She knew too well what price a child paid when parents were thoughtless.

Trey opened the car door for Caitlin and waited until she slid behind the wheel before he jogged across the street to his parked truck.

The house Analisa's mother rented was on the outskirts of town, an old, unkempt building that was dark and unwelcoming. Trey pulled his truck into the driveway behind Caitlin's little sports car and walked up the drive to join them on the sagging porch.

Analisa bent and took a key from beneath the doormat to unlock the door, then pushed it open. She stepped inside, the adults following her.

"My stuff's in my bedroom." She hesitated and looked at Caitlin. "What should I take?"

"Your clothes and your toothbrush, and anything else you think you can't live without for the next day or so."

"Oh."

She hesitated, a frown drawing a tiny line between the arches of her pale, reddish-brown eyebrows.

"What should I put them in?"

"Trey and I will put them in an empty grocery bag."

"Okay." Analisa nodded and turned away.

Caitlin's gaze followed Analisa's small figure as she disappeared through a door on the far side of the room. She shivered and rubbed her arms. "It's cold in here."

"Yeah," Trey agreed. "I wonder if her mother conveniently forgot to pay her heating bill before she left town."

"I don't know, but I'd like to have two minutes alone with that woman," Caitlin said fiercely.

"You'll have to wait in line," Trey said grimly. He glanced around the threadbare room. "Let's see if we can find a sack of some kind."

He took Caitlin's hand and drew her with him across the room and into the kitchen.

The worn linoleum was dull and scuffed but clean, as was the chipped porcelain sink. Trey pulled open overhead cupboards while Caitlin searched below. The shelves were nearly empty. Trey found a half-full jar of instant coffee and some tea bags, and Caitlin discovered a bottle of gin beneath the sink.

"There's not a damn thing for that kid to eat in here," Trey snarled.

The scene was all too familiar—the empty food cupboards, the half-empty bottle of gin and the cold, silent house. He'd never expected to become a father, had never thought he wanted to be. But now that Caitlin carried their child in her body, he was fiercely determined to keep them all safe from the nightmares of neglect, loneliness and despair that had haunted his childhood.

Caitlin took a folded brown paper grocery bag from beneath the sink and straightened. "At least we found something to hold her clothes." She paused on her way toward the living room and pulled open the refrigerator door. The racks inside held only mustard and catsup, a half-empty jar of mayonnaise and a half-full bottle of red wine. "It seems the missing Ms. Watkins likes gin and wine," she commented. She looked at Trey. "I'm calling the police to let them know that we have Analisa, and then I'm going to demand that they file a report. I want this woman charged with child abandonment. And tomorrow, I'm going to the nearest social welfare agency and insist that they look into Analisa's situation. This woman is unfit to care for a child."

"I couldn't agree more," Trey said.

For one brief moment, bitterness and anger blazed from his eyes. Caitlin caught her breath at the glimpse of stark pain that laid bare childhood wounds that were soul-deep. Then he lowered his lashes, glanced away. When he looked back, his green eyes were once again unreadable. This time it was Caitlin who caught his hand in hers and drew him into the living room.

"I'll be right back," she told Trey, and disappeared into the bedroom.

Moments later, she emerged with Analisa's hand tucked firmly in hers and the bulging sack of clothing clutched to her chest. Trey recognized the militant look in her eye, and his anger fled, replaced by amused affection. Caitlin had clearly claimed Analisa Watkins as her own, just as she had done with assorted stray dogs and lost critters when she was a child.

"Ready to go?" he asked mildly.

"Yes." Caitlin marched across the room to the front door.

"Caitlin?"

Caitlin paused and looked into the little girl's worried face. "Yes?"

"The note. We have to leave a note for my mom."

"Oh, yes. The note. I almost forgot." She turned to Trey. "Will you tack a note to the outside of the door?"

"Sure. No problem." Trey patted his jacket and shirt pockets. "Um, do you have something to write on?"

"Yes." Caitlin dug in her purse and produced a pen and a small pad of paper.

"Thanks." He sat on the edge of the sofa and bent over the battered coffee table, pen in hand.

"We'll go on," Caitlin told him. "You're coming to dinner tonight, aren't you?"

"Sure." Trey glanced up, his gaze meeting hers. "I wouldn't miss it for the world."

"Good."

"My truck's blocking your car," he told her. "Give me a second, and I'll be right there."

"All right. I'll tuck Analisa and her things into the car."

Satisfied with the quick flash of heated response he'd seen in Caitlin's eyes, Trey quickly finished scribbling the note. He purposely left the contents brief, telling Ms. Watkins to contact the police for information as to Analisa's whereabouts.

Outside, the wind had kicked up, and Trey hunched his shoulders against its cold bite. Once again he searched his pockets, but they yielded nothing to tack the note to the weathered door, so he folded the paper and closed it in the door, leaving a section of the lined notepaper clearly visible from the outside. Then he loped down the driveway to Caitlin's car. He tapped on the window, and she rolled it down so she could hear him.

He handed her the pen and pad of paper and glanced into the back seat at Analisa. "See you later, Analisa. You can tell me some more about how you managed to ride Caitlin's mare without a saddle or bridle."

"All right," she answered.

Her face was solemn, the chocolate brown eyes faintly apprehensive. Trey grinned at her, and she smiled shyly at him.

His gaze flicked to Caitlin's face, and he felt an overwhelming need to touch her. Ignoring the voice that told him not to, he leaned down and brushed her mouth with his. "And you can tell me if you want to see a movie or go dancing tonight."

"You mean I get to choose?" she asked, her voice husky.

"Sure. I'd prefer dancing, but if you'd rather see a movie, that's fine with me."

Caitlin knew exactly why he'd prefer dancing. Holding each other while swaying to music on a dance floor was infinitely appealing—and infinitely dangerous. She smiled and began to roll up her window. "I'll decide by tonight," she told him. The window reached the top, and she waggled her fingers at him. He smiled wryly, one corner of his mouth kicking up, before he turned and strolled to his truck.

The following morning, as Caitlin sat in the waiting room of the social welfare office, she reflected on the night she'd spent with Trey.

She'd chosen a movie over dancing, but sitting next to Trey in a darkened theater had turned out to be a test of her willpower. He'd stolen heart-shuddering kisses and tucked her hand beneath his on his hard thigh while they shared popcorn. He was eroding her determination piece by tiny piece.

"Miss Drummond?"

The receptionist startled Caitlin, and she jumped, glancing up to find the young woman holding open a door.

"Mrs. Harrington can see you now."

"Thank you." Caitlin gathered her purse, stood and followed the receptionist down the hallway to an inner office.

The brunette behind the cluttered desk stood as Caitlin entered. She held out her hand. "Miss Drummond?" At Caitlin's nod, she smiled. "I'm Janice Harrington." She shook Caitlin's hand and gestured toward a chair facing her desk. "Please, have a seat."

"Thank you." Caitlin sat, placing her shoulder bag on the floor next to the chair.

"Marisa tells me that you have information about an abandoned child?"

"Yes, a little girl named Analisa Watkins." The social worker gave a resigned sigh, and Caitlin paused. "You're familiar with her?"

"Unfortunately, yes." Janice Harrington swung her chair around and pulled open a filing cabinet, then thumbed swiftly through manila folders before pulling one free. She swung back to her desk and flipped open the file. She glanced at Caitlin and gestured at the moderately thick file on her desktop. "As you can see, we already have a growing file."

"Yes, I see. Well." Caitlin drew a deep breath and said bluntly, "We found Analisa shoplifting food at the grocery store yesterday and took her home with us."

"I'm sure there's more to the story," the woman commented.

"Yes. Quite a bit more." Caitlin related the events involving Analisa, starting with the first glimpse of her atop Christmas Girl in the isolated pasture. "So you see," she concluded, "we're very concerned about this child. And we don't want her returned to her mother—not if there's anything humanly and legally possible to prevent it."

"Whether or not she's returned to her mother's custody will have to be determined by the courts. But in the meantime, it seems clear that Analisa has been abandoned by her only known parent, which allows my office to place the child in foster care on an emergency basis without obtaining her mother's permission. Are you and the Hightowers willing to have Analisa remain with you while I do a case study and attempt to locate her mother?"

"Absolutely," Caitlin answered promptly.

"Excellent. We have a shortage of foster homes. If you and your aunt hadn't been willing to have her stay with you, I would probably have to send her out of county."

"That would be devastating for her," Caitlin said, concerned. "I gather from our conversations that she and her mother have moved quite often. Because of the moves, she's been to several schools and is just beginning to feel comfortable in Butte Creek Elementary. She's a bright little girl and genuinely likes her teacher and the other children in her class. If you moved her out of the county, she'd not only be living with a strange family, but she would have new teachers, new classmates, also. It would be overwhelming.''

''Fortunately, that doesn't appear to be necessary,'' Mrs. Harrington said reassuringly. ''Not if she can stay with you and the Hightowers while we look into the whereabouts of her mother. Did Analisa shed any light on when we might expect Lucinda Watkins to return?''

''No, she didn't know.'' Caitlin frowned in frustration. ''I'll be honest with you. I worked with Seattle street kids for several years, and I've never seen a more flagrant case of parental irresponsibility in my life.''

''That's Lucinda,'' the social worker said dryly. She tapped her pencil against the thick file. ''I have a dozen or more reports from Analisa's teachers and concerned neighbors. I investigated and made home visits for each incident, but couldn't find any concrete evidence that would stand up in a court of law, until now.'' Her gaze sharpened. ''You've worked with troubled children?''

''Yes. I was a professor at the University of Washington and published a study of juveniles living on the street in Seattle.''

''How interesting.'' Mrs. Harrington leaned forward, her hands clasped atop her desk. ''Tell me more. How did you happen to choose that specific topic?''

For the next forty-five minutes, Caitlin talked about her experiences with children. The receptionist rang

Mrs. Harrington several times, and each time, the social worker put her off. Finally, the young woman knocked on the door and peered into the office.

"I'm sorry, Mrs. Harrington, but your eleven-thirty appointment has been waiting for ten minutes and says he has another appointment that he can't miss."

"All right, Marisa, tell him I'll be right with him." The girl disappeared, and the social worker turned to Caitlin. "We desperately need people with your experience in the county, Caitlin, not only as children's advocacy volunteers but also to fill the two vacancies we currently have for social workers. I don't know what your plans are, but I hope you'll seriously consider coming to work for us in some capacity if you decide to remain in Butte Creek."

"I have been thinking about the possibility of moving back to Butte Creek to stay," Caitlin confessed. "But I'd thought of looking for employment in education—which is really my field of expertise. I hadn't really considered social work."

"Please do," Janice said sincerely. She stood as Caitlin did and rounded the desk to walk her to the reception area. "We urgently need people with your background, and most especially, with your passion for children's rights."

"I'll think about it. I really will." Caitlin shook the woman's hand and left the office building.

On the way to her car, Caitlin mulled over the proposition. Janice Harrington's suggestion was appealing. Caitlin hadn't considered social work, but working directly with children was a real interest. She loved teaching, but making a difference in even one child's life was so much more fulfilling than lecturing. During the drive home, she grew more and more excited at the prospect.

Watching Analisa and Samantha romp with Max on the living room rug that evening, Caitlin's conviction that Janice Harrington had the perfect solution to her dilemma grew stronger. Analisa seemed content to be staying with the Hightowers, and Caitlin felt a deep sense of satisfaction that her and Trey's intervention had made a difference in the little girl's life.

No one intervened for Trey until he was fifteen years old. The thought was sobering. Surely being cared for by Lucas Hightower had been welcome sanctuary for the teenager, but how much damage had the years with his mother done to Trey? The winter-cold bleakness in his eyes had been stark testimony that he'd never forgotten those early years. Would he ever? Could a man who had been deeply damaged in childhood learn to love as an adult? Could he give his heart to a wife and baby?

Caitlin didn't know the answers to her questions. And she was very afraid that unless she could find them, Trey's heart would remain forever locked away.

Chapter Seven

The phone rang in the Hightower kitchen, and Caitlin lifted the receiver, then tucked it between her ear and shoulder and dried her hands. She kept a watchful eye on Samantha, Justin and Analisa, who'd been with them a full week.

"Hello?" she answered.

"Hello, is Caitlin Drummond in?"

"Yes, speaking."

The female voice warmed. "Caitlin, this is Janice Harrington at Social Services."

"Hello, Janice."

"I'm calling about Analisa. Her mother came into the office earlier today."

Caitlin quickly checked that the two girls were busy peeling carrots and Justin was chopping onions, before stepping around the corner into the living room.

"Yes?"

"She went to Las Vegas with her boyfriend on vacation, and while they were there the two got married."

"So Analisa has a new stepfather to deal with." Caitlin wondered how the little girl felt about her mother's boyfriend-turned-husband.

"No, she won't, fortunately."

"She won't?"

"No, she won't. That's the good news. It's also the bad news."

"I don't understand." Caitlin peered around the corner. The girls were chatting and giggling. Justin had turned up the volume of the pop music coming from the radio on the shelf beside him. It added enough noise to drown out Caitlin's voice. "What did Mrs. Watkins say?"

"At first she demanded that I tell her where Analisa was staying and to return her immediately. When I told Lucinda that her daughter was in foster care and would stay there until we reviewed her home and until the court decided whether to charge Lucinda with child abandonment, she calmed down and wanted to bargain. The interview ended with Lucinda signing over custody of Analisa to the State of Montana. I believe her words were, 'The kid's always been an anchor around my neck. You can have her. I'm starting a new life in Vegas with Gus'."

"Oh, no." Caitlin closed her eyes against the relief that vied with a wave of sympathy for Analisa.

"I told you, it's good news and bad news. The good news is Analisa will no longer be subject to her mother's carelessness. But the bad news is she's forced to deal with being abandoned by her mother again, this time for good."

Caitlin's heart ached for Analisa. She knew all too well the pain caused by a mother's indifference. Her mother had had a succession of men friends—most of whom didn't want Caitlin around. When she was twelve, her mother's current boyfriend had threatened and then hit her. With bruises and black eye, she'd stuffed a change of clothes in her backpack and hitch-hiked from Los Angeles to Aunt Sarah's home in Montana. She'd never gone back, choosing to remain with Sarah and Josh in Butte Creek, but her mother had visited and kept in touch in the years since, and they'd reached a truce of sorts. She couldn't imagine how much more painful it would have been if Margaret Drummond had signed her over to the state and deserted her.

"...be a problem?"

"I'm sorry." Caitlin realized that Janice Harrington had continued speaking, and she hadn't heard a word. "I'm afraid I didn't catch that."

"I asked if Analisa could remain with you and the Hightowers for a few more days while I try to find a more permanent foster home for her."

"How difficult is it to qualify as a foster home?" Caitlin asked slowly, her gaze fixed on Analisa's solemn face, the pink tip of her tongue caught between her teeth as she concentrated fiercely on the half-peeled carrot in her hand. Max lay at her feet, his chin resting on the toe of her scuffed tennis shoe, his gaze fastened unwaveringly on the strips curling away from the peeler.

"That depends. Are you thinking of applying?"

"I'd love to, but at the moment, I don't have a home of my own." *And I'll be having a baby soon. Can I be a good mother to two children?* "I'd like to ask Sarah and Josh if Analisa can stay here at the ranch permanently. I hate the thought of her being moved to a strange home. I'm really concerned about the effect it would have on her to have to deal with a new family at the same time she's coming to terms with her mother's desertion."

"I'm concerned about that, also," Janice agreed. "And it's possible that I may not be able to find a vacancy in the Butte Creek school district, which would mean that she would be moved to a new school."

"Can you give me a day or two to discuss this with Sarah and Josh?" Caitlin asked.

"Absolutely. It will take me that long to process the legal documents."

"And I'd like to talk to my aunt and uncle before telling Analisa about her mother. I think it would be easier for her if she's told what will happen to her next when she learns her mother is gone. Do you see any problem with the delay?"

"Not if it's only for a day or two."

"Great." Caitlin drew a deep breath. "I'll call you by the day after tomorrow at the latest, and we can discuss what happens next."

"Sounds good. I'll expect to hear from you then."

Caitlin said goodbye to the social worker and walked into the kitchen to hang the receiver on its wall-mounted base.

"Who was on the phone, Caitee?"

"Just a friend. How are you two coming with those carrots?"

"We're almost done."

"Caitlin, did you know that Max likes to eat carrot peels?" Analisa asked, glancing at the little dog at her feet.

Caitlin chuckled. "Max likes to eat *anything,*" she responded. "The only thing I've ever given him that he refused to eat were mushrooms."

"Really?" Analisa carefully placed the last carrot in the pot, wiped her hands on her apron and bent to stroke the dachshund's silky head. "Is that true, Maxie?" she crooned.

The little dog responded by lifting his ears and barking, two short, sharp yaps.

Analisa beamed at Caitlin. "He understands me! And he talks back."

"I sometimes suspect that Max understands English better than some humans," Caitlin said wryly. She tucked a strand of hair behind her ear and planted her hands on her hips, scanning the kitchen. "Okay, guys, where were we?"

"You were chopping the onions," Justin said, wiping his sleeve across his watering eyes. "Then you went off and left me with them."

"And Analisa and I finished peeling the carrots, so we get to have cookies and tea." Samantha chimed in.

"Sorry about the onions, Justin, but thanks for finishing them for me. I owe you." Caitlin lifted a questioning eyebrow at Samantha. "And what's this about cookies and tea? I thought it was a cookie, as in *one* cookie, and a glass of milk?"

"But you're going to have tea, aren't you?"

"Yes."

"And you always drink herbal tea, which doesn't have caffeine, so we can have it too, right? Please." Samantha wrapped her hands around Caitlin's waist and hugged her.

"All right, but don't tell your mother that I gave you tea instead of milk."

"We won't."

Samantha skipped across the room and pulled the cookie jar from the back of the counter, took a plate from the cabinet above and piled it high with chocolate cookies. Justin reached over her head and snagged two of them.

The outer door slammed, followed by the shuffle of boots and the sound of voices that grew louder when the door from the utility room opened.

"Hi, Daddy," Samantha called.

"Hi, kiddo." Josh dropped a kiss atop Samantha's blond head and smiled gently at Analisa. "What are you two girls up to?"

"We're helping Caitee make dinner."

"We peeled carrots," Analisa added softly.

"And now we're having tea and a cookie," Caitlin added. Sarah and Trey had entered the room and stood behind Josh. "Sorry, Sarah, I know they should be drinking milk, but I promised Samantha that she and Analisa could have tea—it's herbal."

"Strawberry," Samantha added.

Trey caught Caitlin's eye and shuddered.

"I'm sure you'd like some strawberry tea, wouldn't you, Trey?"

"Thanks, but I think I'll pass on the tea. Is there any coffee?" he asked hopefully.

"Yes, of course. Have you ever found the coffee-pot empty in this house?"

"Now that you mention it, no, I don't think I ever have." Trey walked behind Caitlin to the cupboard where the mugs were kept, resisting the urge to stroke her fanny as he passed. She was wearing a loose, cream tunic sweater over black leggings, and the sweater clung to her body, cupping the curve of her bottom. He wondered if she thought the loose sweater was concealing and if he should tell her that it made her soft curves damn near irresistible.

His palms itched to touch her, but he resolutely ignored the impulse, took a mug from the cupboard and poured coffee. He turned to walk to the table and was jolted by the expression on Caitlin's face as she gazed at Analisa, seated across the room at the table with Samantha, Justin, Sarah and Josh. Caitlin's green eyes were shadowed, and tension drew tiny lines between her brows. He cupped her elbow, and she looked at him.

"Is something wrong?" he asked softly, his lips brushing the soft shell of her ear.

"I'll tell you later," she murmured.

"How was school today?" Sarah asked as Trey and Caitlin took seats at the table where the two girls were pouring tea from the rosebud china pot into matching cups.

"Same old thing," Justin mumbled around a mouthful of cookie.

"It was okay." Samantha wrinkled her nose. "But I have math homework tonight. Will you help me, Daddy?"

"Sure, right after dinner."

"Speaking of dinner," Caitlin began. "When you two girls are finished with your tea, will you and Justin take Max outside for some exercise before it's time to eat?"

"Sure." Never willing to sit still for long, Samantha drained her teacup in one long swig and stood. "I'm ready."

Analisa followed her example and slid off her chair. "Me, too."

Samantha reached for the cookie plate, but Sarah shook her head.

"Only one more, young lady, or you'll be too full to eat your dinner."

"All right. Here, Analisa." Samantha handed a cookie to the younger girl. "Great cookies, Mom. Thanks."

"You're welcome." Sarah smiled indulgently as her daughter left the room, Analisa in tow, Max bouncing along beside them. Justin strolled in their wake.

The back door slammed moments later, and the sound of the girls' laughter mingled with Max's barking and Justin's voice.

"I don't know how that little dog of yours keeps up with those kids, Caitlin," Josh said, tilting his chair back.

"They're good for him," Caitlin responded, turning her cup in slow half-circles on the tabletop. "I used to worry about whether he was getting enough exercise in Seattle—especially when I had to work late and didn't have time to take him for a long walk before bed. I'm sure this is his version of doggy heaven." Abruptly, she abandoned her teacup and folded her hands. "I need to talk to all of you about something."

Trey tensed. Had she made a decision about marrying him?

"Janice Harrington called today. She's the social worker that I talked to about Analisa."

His muscles loosened, and Trey realized that he'd been holding his breath. He exhaled slowly and took a sip of coffee.

"Lucinda Watkins returned from vacation—she went to Las Vegas and married her boyfriend. Evidently she found your note when she got back, Trey, and the sheriff must have sent her to the social services office. Janice told me that given the possibility of being charged with child abandonment, Lucinda decided to give up her parental rights and leave the state.''

Trey swore under his breath, his jaw tight with anger. Josh's eyes snapped with outrage, and Sarah's expressive features reflected shock and dismay.

''Well, at least we don't have to worry about that idiotic woman leaving the kid alone in a cold house without food again,'' Trey growled.

''Yes, but now that poor little girl will be shuffled into foster care.'' Sarah shoved her fingers through her shoulder-length blond hair and shook her head.

''Janice asked if Analisa could stay here for a day or two while she tries to find a placement for her.''

Sarah glanced at Josh, communicating silently. ''Absolutely,'' Josh said firmly.

''Good. There's something else.... I'd like to ask you to consider letting her stay here permanently.'' Caitlin caught the glance her aunt and uncle shared and hurried to explain. ''It's going to be devastating enough for her to cope with being deserted forever by her mother. She's only just begun to get used to us. I'm afraid that if she's shifted to a strange family now, she'll never trust adults again, and that could lead to so many problems for her in the future. I can't tell you how many girls I saw on the streets in Seattle who'd become Ping-Pong balls in the foster system.''

''I don't know, Caitlin,'' Sarah said. ''Josh and I need to discuss this.''

''She can live with us, Caitlin.''

Caitlin's gaze flew to Trey. ''You'd do that? Take

in a ten-year-old girl you hardly know?'' she asked, shaken by the conviction in his eyes.

''She reminds me of you when you first came to Butte Creek,'' he said simply. ''She needs someone to feed her and keep her safe. We can do that.''

Like Lucas kept me safe. Like Sarah and Josh kept you safe, Caitlin.

He didn't say the words. He didn't have to. Caitlin read them in his eyes, in the implacable set of his jaw, and tears welled in her eyes, clogged her throat. Impulsively, she reached across the table and covered his hand with hers. He turned his hand palm up and threaded his fingers between hers, binding them together.

''Analisa will stay with us,'' Sarah said, breaking the silence that gripped the room. ''At least until the two of you reach some decision about your own future.''

''Thank you.'' Her aunt's words reminded Caitlin that Analisa couldn't live with her and Trey unless they were married and shared a home that could include her. One more reason added to the need to resolve her concerns about marrying Trey. ''Do you think we could call her in and tell her? I don't think I'll be able to sleep until we do.''

''Sure.'' Josh rose and went to the back door to call the children.

They returned to the house quickly, and Samantha patted Analisa's shoulder, her eyes worried and sympathetic, when her father asked her and Justin to go into the living room while the adults talked to Analisa. Analisa's chocolate brown eyes were wary, her face pale as she took a seat at the table. Although she didn't cry when they explained what her mother had done, Caitlin didn't miss the flinch as if her slight body had taken a blow. And she wasn't at all sure the little girl believed Sarah and Josh would keep her at the ranch. The child was stoic and dry-eyed, sitting quietly through dinner while she pretended to eat but only moved food from one side of her plate to the other. Caitlin was worried about her, but Analisa continued to repeat that she was fine.

The children had long since gone to their beds when Caitlin walked Trey to the door just after ten-thirty.

''Come outside with me for a few minutes.''

''It's cold out there.''

''I'll keep you warm,'' he murmured, his gaze dropping to her mouth.

''Trey Weber, are you trying to seduce me?'' she asked, her voice throaty.

''I wish,'' he drawled with feeling. He took her coat from the closet and tucked her into it before he pulled her outside and down the steps to his truck. He yanked open the passenger side door, lifted her onto the seat and slid in after her, then closed them inside. ''Damn, it's cold in here,'' he said and leaned past her to move the gearshift into neutral and turn the key. The heater blew cold air into the cab.

''Yikes. That's freezing!'' Caitlin scooted away from the air vent and straight into the solid wall of Trey's chest.

He didn't mind. He tightened his arms around her and hauled her across his lap.

"I told you—I'll be glad to keep you warm," he said.

Caitlin sighed and gave herself up to the hot magic of his mouth and the erotic pleasure of his hands beneath her sweater. Her breasts were so sensitive that the faintest brush of his callused fingertips against her nipples sent rivers of sensation coursing through her body to throb between her legs. His hand left her breast and smoothed down her back to cup the curve of her bottom.

He lifted his mouth from hers a fraction.

"I'm crazy about your breasts," he muttered. "But you have no idea what this sweater does to your..."

The last word was unintelligible. Caitlin opened her eyes and looked at him. The flames that flickered in his eyes grew hotter with each petting stroke of his hand over her bottom.

"What did you say?" she asked drowsily, mesmerized by his eyes, breathless from the stroking of his hand, his open mouth on her skin and the hard heat of his body beneath her.

"When?" he whispered, distracted by her taste on his tongue.

"Just now."

He lifted his head, shook it slightly and stared at her, confused. "Just now, what?"

"You said something about my sweater."

"Your sweater?" His gaze flickered down her body and fastened on the cream wool. His hand was beneath it, cupping the sweet curve of her bottom. He flexed his fingers, pressing her tighter against him. "Oh, yeah. Your sweater. It turns me on."

She blinked at his blunt statement. "This baggy thing?"

"You may think it's baggy, honey, but it clings in all the right places. All I could think about tonight was getting my hands under it and on you."

"Trey!" Her cheeks, flushed from his lovemaking, turned warmer.

"Sorry, honey, but it's the truth. When I'm with you, I rarely think of much else. Don't you think about being with me?"

Caitlin caught her breath. His blue eyes demanded honesty. "Yes," she admitted, smoothing her hand over his cheek, down his throat to the pulse that pounded fiercely at the base, before moving beneath the opening of his shirt. "I think about being with you a lot. I miss you, Trey."

The stark honesty of her words ripped into him.

"Oh, honey, I miss you, too." He kissed her, nearly over the edge with the need to have her. He eased lower in the seat, craving the feel of her soft body lying atop his. His knee banged painfully against the steering wheel, and he groaned. "Damn." He swore feelingly and sat up, holding Caitlin tightly when she would have shifted off his lap. "Why are we necking in a truck like a couple of teenagers when I've got a perfectly good bed at home?"

She didn't answer, and he sighed, dropping his head against the headrest to stare at the ceiling.

"I'll walk you back to the house," he said, and reached for the door handle.

"Trey...I'm sorry. Maybe we shouldn't be doing this."

"Hey." He laid a finger against her lips. "I'd love it if you'd come home with me and finish what we've started. But I promised that I wouldn't pressure you. And as for 'this'—" he kissed her sweetly "—I don't want to give up touching you. I can live with necking in the truck and freezing showers. For a while."

"All right."

He walked her to the door and left her with another hot kiss that melted her bones and made her question whether her determination to hear Trey say "I love you" before they were married was really relevant.

But by the time she'd washed her face, brushed her teeth, given her hair its nightly hundred strokes and tumbled exhausted into bed, she was once again sure that she needed to hear Trey speak the words. He needed to say them, she thought sleepily, just as much as she needed to hear them.

A noise awakened Caitlin just before midnight. Confused, she sat up and squinted at the clock. The soft noise came again, and she pushed back the covers and left her bed to open the door to the hall. The sound was much fainter. Frowning, Caitlin turned to search her bedroom. The door to her closet stood ajar, and she moved across the room to close it before returning to bed. As her hand closed over the knob, the noise came again, this time louder.

Sobs? Someone's crying in my closet?

She pulled the door wider and stared into the interior. There was no one there—only her clothing, shoes and hats. Puzzled, Caitlin frowned until it dawned on her that Samantha's room was next door and their closets were back to back.

Caitlin quickly left her room and quietly entered the bedroom next to hers. The night-light illuminated the room with a faint glow, and it was easy to see that only one little girl mounded the covers on the big bed. Caitlin walked silently to the closet and pulled open the door.

Analisa was crouched on the floor, huddled in a blanket, her thin body shuddering with the sobs she tried unsuccessfully to muffle. She lifted her tear-streaked face, her eyes swimming with hopelessness.

It broke Caitlin's heart.

''Oh, sweetheart,'' she murmured helplessly. She bent and caught the too-thin little girl in her arms and lifted her to her feet. She was too big for Caitlin to carry, but carry her she did, the child's legs dangling and bumping against her thighs as she took the little girl to her room, nudging the door softly closed with her elbow. She climbed into bed without releasing Analisa, who was still clutching her blanket, and she rocked her comfortingly. ''Hush. It's all right, Analisa. It's going to be all right. I promise.''

''No, it's n-n-not,'' she wailed.

''Yes, everything's going to be fine. I promise you it will.''

Analisa continued to cry in deep, harsh sobs that

racked her body. Caitlin held her close and crooned, mentally cursing Lucinda Watkins.

"Honey, you're going to make yourself sick if you keep this up."

The only response was another deep sob. The child's grief was heartbreaking to hear. Caitlin rocked her, for long moments until at last she quieted and only an occasional sob shuddered through her.

"My mom doesn't want me."

Caitlin didn't know what to say. But she knew that she couldn't lie to the child, so she gave Lucinda Watkins the benefit of the doubt.

"I don't believe for a minute that your mother doesn't want you. But sometimes adults make mistakes. They lose track of what's really important and make choices that they later regret. Sometimes they think their choices are best for their children, and sometimes the children don't agree."

Caitlin could almost hear the wheels turning as Analisa considered her words.

"Why would it be best for me for my mom to go away?"

"I don't know, Analisa. But I do know that she left you in good hands, because Sarah and Josh and Justin and Samantha are so glad to have you here. And so am I. And Trey is looking forward to having you show him how you learned to ride bareback so well."

"Will I get to stay here always?" Her voice was barely a whisper in the dark room.

"We're going to do everything we can to keep you," Caitlin told her. "Mrs. Harrington is going to visit and talk to all of us about your living with us. Do you remember Mrs. Harrington?''

''Yes.'' Analisa nodded, her tangled curls brushing against Caitlin's throat and the underside of her chin. ''She came to see my mom a couple of times. I don't think my mom liked her.''

''Really? Why not?''

''I don't know. I thought Mrs. Harrington was nice, but my mom was mad after she left.''

''Hmm. Well, I think you're right. Mrs. Harrington is very nice. And I know that she'll do everything she can to make sure that you're happy. Would it make you happy to stay here at the ranch?''

''Yes.'' The little girl's voice was soft but very definite. ''I like it here. I like having my own room, and everybody's nice to me. And I love Max.'' Her body stiffened, her fingers clutching the sleeve of Caitlin's nightshirt. ''Will you be here?''

''Yes.'' Caitlin hugged her closer. ''I'm not going anywhere.''

''But Samantha said that you live in Seattle and you're only visiting.''

''I did live in Seattle, but I'm going to stay in Butte Creek from now on.''

''Okay.'' Her voice was calmer.

Caitlin tilted her head to look at Analisa. The child's eyes were heavy-lidded with exhaustion, her body slowly going boneless as she edged toward sleep. ''Why don't you curl up in here with me.'' Caitlin pulled the blankets back and eased the little girl off her lap and onto the sheet. ''There we go.

Here, give me the blanket.'' She tugged the blanket carefully from under Analisa and watched with relief as the little girl snuggled her face into the pillow, already nearly asleep.

''Good night,'' she whispered, brushing tangled red curls from the girl's face before bending to drop a quick kiss against her tear-dampened cheek.

'''Night.'' Analisa's response was a drowsy murmur.

Caitlin pulled the blankets up, tucked them around Analisa's shoulders and lay beside her staring at the shadowy ceiling. Outside her bedroom window, a limb of the big elder tree that shaded the side of the house rubbed against the siding as the wind picked up, the scratching noise familiar and somehow comforting in the dark night.

She remembered vividly being twelve years old and realizing that she had to leave her mother's home. What would have become of her if Sarah and Josh hadn't been willing to take her in?

She turned her head on the pillow and looked at Analisa's pale face and the mop of curly red hair, dark against the white pillowcase.

We'll keep you safe, she vowed silently.

The days settled into a routine. Caitlin contacted Janice Harrington and arranged for a home visit. While Janice was processing the Hightowers' application for approval as a foster home, she also convinced Caitlin to accept a part-time volunteer position as a counselor with the agency. Janice was bluntly honest in telling her that she hoped Caitlin would decide to accept a permanent paid position. Knowing she didn't want to work until after her baby was born, Caitlin would only promise to consider the possibility.

Busy with the volunteer work and her horses, Caitlin was hardly aware that the days flowed into weeks and the weeks into a month, until it was mid-November and she woke one morning to find that the first serious snowfall of the winter season had left a foot of snow on the ground during the night.

Justin, Samantha and Analisa pelted each other with snowballs on their way to the bus stop at the end of the lane. Caitlin and Sarah watched them from the living room window, laughing when the two girls joined forces to shower the older Justin with a flurry of snowballs.

''If they keep that up, they'll be soaking wet before they even get on the bus.'' Sarah shook her head and turned to her dusting.

''Ah, the smell of wet wool in the schoolroom.'' Caitlin rolled her eyes in mock appreciation, earning a laugh from Sarah. Carrying her mug of tea, she headed for the stairs. ''I'm going upstairs to make my bed. I'll check the kids' rooms and the bathrooms for any stray dirty laundry and toss it in the washer with mine before I leave for Uncle Wes's. Is there anything else you want me to do before I leave?''

''No, thanks. I'm going to finish up here and run over to CeCe's for the day. She's going to give me another weaving lesson.''

"Okay."

Caitlin was gathering wet towels from the upstairs bathroom when Sarah called from the bottom of the stairs.

"Caitlin?"

"Yes?" She dropped the towels on the bathroom floor and walked to the end of the hall. Sarah stood at the foot of the stairs, dressed in a heavy winter coat, gloves and hat.

"I just wanted to let you know that I'm leaving now. I probably won't be home until the kids are due from the bus."

"Okay. Have fun."

"You, too. Tell Wes and Molly Hi for me."

"I will. Bye."

Sarah left the house, and Caitlin went to the bathroom to empty the hamper and gather the wet towels before she swept the pile into her arms and headed downstairs to the utility room. The washing machine was humming gently when she pulled on her boots and shrugged into her heavy coat. She was tucking her hair into a green knit hat when someone knocked on the back door. Startled, she pushed the curtain aside to find Trey on the back step. Immediately she pulled open the door.

"Hi," she said, delighted to see him. "I didn't hear your truck drive up."

"That's because I didn't drive over in the truck." His gaze swiftly took in her outer clothing, and he nodded in satisfaction. "Good. You're wearing warm clothes."

"Yes." She glanced at her coat and boots, then to him. "I'm on my way over to Wes's to check on the horses. Why?"

"I have a surprise for you," he said, catching her hand and drawing her outside, closing the door behind them. "And you need to be bundled up so you don't get cold."

Puzzled, she glanced around but saw nothing that explained his statement. "Really? What is it?"

"You'll see. Close your eyes and come with me."

He kept her hand clasped in his and led her to the front of the house.

She stumbled, grabbed his forearm with her free hand in a bid for balance and laughingly protested. "Trey! I can't see where I'm going! Don't let me fall down."

"I won't." He continued to lead her.

Caitlin heard the snow crunch against concrete beneath her boots and knew she was being led down the sidewalk in front of the house. Impossible though it seemed, she thought she could hear the jingle and tinkle of bells.

"Curiosity is killing me, Trey. Can't I look yet?"

"No. Not yet—but soon."

She struggled to keep up with his longer strides, the snow crunching under their boots, the crisp air filling her lungs.

He stopped abruptly. "All right. You can open your eyes now."

She lifted her eyes and blinked, trying to adjust to the glitter of sunlight off white snow. She gasped.

"Oh, Trey." It was all she could manage to say. Her eyes widened in astonished delight. Not six feet away was an old-fashioned sleigh, its runners gleaming with new paint, the body bright red with gold trim. A black mare stood between the traces, its harness of black leather polished to a high sheen, the breast collar studded with small silver bells that jingled musically each time the horse shifted, stamped her foot or switched her tail.

Caitlin was enchanted, and she stroked her gloved palm along the sleek crimson surface of the painted sleigh. A heavy navy-blue wool throw was tossed on the seat, and she shifted it aside, sighing over the buttoned black leather beneath.

"It's absolutely gorgeous," she breathed, glancing over her shoulder. Trey stood with his arms crossed, an affectionate half smile curving his lips, clearly pleased with her response. She glanced at the horse and sleigh. "And it's just exactly like the sleigh I used to dream about when we were kids. Do you remember?"

"I remember," he confirmed. "The first Christmas after you came to live in Montana, Josh gave Sarah a copy of the classic movie, *White Christmas.* You and Sarah made us watch it with you every night for a week until we knew the dialogue by heart. And you swore that when you grew up, you were going to teach *me* to sing like Bing Crosby, *you* were going to learn to dance like Vera Ellen, and *we* were going to own a red-and-gold sleigh to ride in every winter.''

''You do remember!'' She glowed with delight. ''Wherever did you find the sleigh?''

''From a rancher east of Scobey. It was stored in his hay barn under a tarp and a pile of old harness bits and pieces.''

''And you restored it?'' At his nod, Caitlin sighed with appreciation and again ran a hand lovingly over the high curve of the front footboard. ''You did a beautiful job, Trey. It's absolutely gorgeous.''

He closed the distance between them and reached past her to toss the wool blanket aside. ''This is the first time I've had it out. I thought you might want to go with me on her trial run.''

''I'd love to.''

Trey caught her waist and lifted her into the sleigh, then he vaulted after her. The seat was comfortably padded and just the right size for two adults. Caitlin spread the blue wool over their laps as Trey unwound the reins.

''Ready?''

''Ready,'' she confirmed.

He slapped the reins against the big mare's back and she stepped forward, the sleigh jerking into motion then sliding smoothly on the thick layer of new snow as the horse trotted out of the barnyard.

''Where are we going?'' The breeze created by

their passing was brisk, quickly turning Caitlin's cheeks pink from the cold. But tucked beneath the heavy wool, with the heat of Trey's hard body pressing against her side from shoulder to hip, thigh to ankle, she was snug and warm.

"I thought we'd cut across the pastures. I didn't want to try the roads on this test run. We can have lunch at my place. I'll drive you home in the truck if you decide it's too cold for you in the sleigh."

"All right." Caitlin tucked her arm through his and settled comfortably, enjoying the crisp, cold air, the sunlight sparkling off the glistening white snow and the jingle of the sleigh bells. "This is just the way I dreamed riding in a sleigh would be," she remarked.

"Yeah?" Trey glanced at her. Her green eyes were misty. He bent and kissed her, her mouth warm and lush beneath his. "Good. I hoped it would be."

The horse trotted briskly, pulling the sleigh with smooth efficiency over the snow-covered pastures. They left Drummond land, cut across the far corner of Lucas Hightower's ranch and entered Trey's pasture.

"I ran cattle here last year," he commented, assessing the state of the barbed wire fence. "But you could summer your horses here if you want. There's a year-round spring just beyond the north end of that butte." He gestured to the south where a long, flat-topped butte rose above the prairie floor.

"I hadn't thought past this winter," Caitlin admitted. ''Is the grass better here than in Uncle Wes's north pasture?''

Trey narrowed his eyes in thought, sweeping the snow-covered acres with a considering glance. ''I doubt that the grass is better here except in the spring, when it stays green until well into the summer. But this pasture is closer to my place than Wes's north pasture.'' His gaze met hers. ''If you decide to marry me, you won't have as far to drive to check on them.''

''Oh. I see.'' She looked over the snow-covered prairie. Would next summer find her married to Trey, their baby between them, her horses pastured on his acres? She desperately wanted it to be true.

When she didn't say anything further, Trey slapped the reins lightly against the mare's flanks, and she picked up her pace. Within a half hour, bells jingling, they arrived at Trey's headquarters, and he pulled the mare to a stop in front of the big barn.

He tossed back the wool throw, swung to the ground, then turned to hold his hands out to Caitlin.

''Come here, sweetheart. I want to run the sleigh into the barn behind the mare. The less weight on the runners when they hit the concrete barn floor, the better.''

Caitlin tucked the blue wool cover onto the seat beside her and slid across the seat before she stood. Trey settled his hands on her waist, and Caitlin bent forward, resting her hands on his shoulders. He picked her up and lifted her easily out of the sleigh before he turned and lowered her slowly, letting her body slide down the front of his.

Her fingers tightened on his jacket. The friction of their bodies was having a decided effect on his body, and hers was reacting with the usual frantic heat.

Trey held her still when her hips reached his waist, her lips nearly even with his.

Suddenly his need to possess this woman overrode his better judgment, and Trey found himself perilously close to breaking the promise he'd made.

Chapter Eight

"Wrap your legs around my waist," he urged, his voice smoky with desire.

Despite her swimming senses, Caitlin held onto sanity.

"I don't think so," she whispered. "I can only deal with a limited amount of temptation, and I've got all I can handle at the moment."

Trey wanted to insist, but then she kissed him, soft, brushing movements of her warm lips across his jaw before her mouth moved up to trace the line of his cheekbone, the corner of his eye. He let his lashes drift closed, and she kissed those, too, gentle, tender kisses that made him feel treasured. And loved.

He opened his eyes, and she drew back to smile at him. She was so beautiful she made his heart ache.

Her green eyes were misty with emotion, her cheeks flushed with pink from the cold, her black hair gleaming beneath the weak winter sunlight. The bright red muffler tucked into the collar of her green winter jacket echoed Caitlin's vivid coloring.

"Thank you for the sleigh," she said softly. "You've made my childhood dream come true. And I know how hard you must have worked."

"Oh, it wasn't much," he murmured, grinning crookedly. "Only a few hundred hours or so. Seeing you smile made it worth every minute of it."

"Really?" Caitlin smiled. She couldn't help it. Tucked deep inside the tough male that was Trey was a sweet, gentle core that melted her heart. "What a sweet thing to say. What a sweet man you are."

"Sweet?" Genuine horror crossed his features. "I am *not* sweet." He glared at her. "Don't ever repeat that in front of my friends."

"Yes, sir." Caitlin bit her lip to keep from laughing.

He frowned and set her on her feet. "I am not sweet," he repeated before he kissed her swiftly, decisively. He strode away from her and caught the mare's reins just behind the bridle to lead her into the barn, the sleigh gliding smoothly behind until the runners hit the concrete barn floor. Then the shiny metal rasped and grated, complaining at the lack of snow to ease its passage.

Caitlin followed, leaning her weight against the heavy door to slide it shut and closing them into the big barn, fragrant with the smell of hay and horses.

"Can I help?"

"Sure." Trey glanced up from the traces. "Give me a minute with this harness, then you can rub Callie dry while I fork hay down."

They worked companionably together, Trey toting the harness into the tack room while Caitlin walked the mare into a stall and rubbed the sweat from her steaming flanks. Trey climbed the wooden ladder into the loft and dropped flakes of hay into the manger before returning to the lower floor to scoop grain from a barrel and pour oats into the other half of the manger. The mare immediately dropped her muzzle into the pile of grain.

Trey rubbed her neck, smoothing the rough black forelock out of her eyes, then he glanced at Caitlin. She was currying the black's coat, stretching to sweep the brush down the length of the mare's spine. He took a curry brush from the box just outside the stall and joined Caitlin, facing her across the mare's back. With both of them grooming the horse, they were quickly finished.

"I'm starving," he said. "Let's see what we can find in the refrigerator." They stepped outside and he started to slide the door closed behind them. The heavy door caught and jammed, refusing to budge. Trey pulled harder. The door didn't move. Impatiently, he put his shoulder against it and shoved hard. The door came loose with a jerk and slid along the track until it slammed against the door jamb. The force of the door hitting the wooden jamb shook the side wall, rattling the metal bracket that supported a big floodlight just below the roof directly above Caitlin. The mound of soft snow that covered the floodlight and bracket came tumbling down—right on Caitlin's head.

She shrieked with surprise.

Trey spun, and his eyes widened. Caitlin was covered in snow. It piled atop her black hair and sifted down her neck inside her coat collar. She'd unbuttoned her coat and unwrapped her muffler in the warmth of the barn, and the snow was a fan of melting white already dampening the front of her sweater and the blue denim covering her thighs and knees. Her surprised, indignant expression was priceless. Trey burst into laughter.

Still stunned, Caitlin held her arms wide and looked at the snow spattering her chest and thighs. Not only was it cold, the dampness was beginning to seep through the fabric and reach her skin. She frowned, looked up and caught Trey howling with laughter. The frown turned into a scowl.

"You think this is funny, do you?"

Trey wiped the back of his hand across his eyes and tried to stop laughing.

"No." He managed to get the word out. But one look at the disbelief and outrage on her face as she glared at the offending bracket and light set him off again.

"You did this on purpose, didn't you?" Suspicion turned to certainty when he burst into laughter at her words, despite the fact that he shook his head, unable to speak for laughing. She narrowed her eyes and contemplated revenge.

Someone had plowed the barnyard, piling the snow beyond the barn, and the four-foot-high bank of soft white beckoned to Caitlin. She caught Trey's forearm and marched him toward the house.

"Come on, laughing boy. We're going in the house so I can get dry."

Still chuckling, the unsuspecting Trey went with her, not even noticing when she veered to the left and pulled him to a halt.

"What?" he asked.

"I owe you one, Weber," she said sweetly, and before he could react, she put her palms against his chest and shoved. He tumbled backward, straight into the snowbank, where he lay spread-eagled, blinking at her.

"You pushed me."

His voice had a disbelieving tone that brought a quick, mischievous grin to Caitlin's face.

"Yes. I did." She bent, scooped up a handful of snow and before he could protect himself, quickly stuffed it down the front of his jacket. He roared with surprise and grabbed her hands, yanking her on top of him and rolling until she was flat on her back in the snow with him straddling her thighs.

"You'll pay for that," he said menacingly. She was giggling too hard to pay attention, so he sank his hand into the snowbank, grabbed a fistful of cold snow and smeared her face with the icy, wet stuff.

She twisted and wriggled under him, her eyes squeezed shut, laughing.

"Trey! Stop! I give up!"

"Are you sorry you attacked me?" he demanded.

"Yes."

"Are you going to do it again?"

She opened her eyes and looked at him. "Yes."

He shook his head. "You're incorrigible."

"Look who's talking!" She squirmed uncomfortably. "Let me up, Trey. This snowbank is cold—and wet."

He stood and pulled her to her feet, then he turned her around to brush the snow from her back. "Geez, woman," he growled. "You're soaking wet."

She glanced over her shoulder at him. Snow was melting in his hair, and the knees of his jeans were soaked through where he'd knelt in the snow. "So are you. Look at your jeans."

"I know, and it's damned uncomfortable." He gave her backside a final swat and leaned over to grab his hat from the snowy ground where it had tumbled when he fell. "Let's go inside and get out of these wet clothes." He caught her hand and pulled her after him, his long strides swiftly eating up the distance between barn and house.

Caitlin half ran to keep up with his longer stride. They entered the utility room off the kitchen, and Trey tugged her jacket from her, scowling as he fingered the wet sweater she wore beneath.

"Your clothes are soaked." He lifted her and set her on top of the washing machine to remove her boots. "I shouldn't have rolled you into that snow-bank," he muttered, dropping her boots on the floor.

"And I shouldn't have pushed you in first," Caitlin commented, unbuttoning his jacket. He stood still and let her. She pushed the edges of the jacket aside and tested the heavy flannel shirt beneath with her fingers. "You're just as wet from the snow I stuffed inside your jacket."

"You're right, and if we both don't get into dry clothes, we're likely to catch pneumonia." Trey caught her by the waist and lifted her down. He shrugged out of his jacket and tossed it on the dryer, dropped his hat on top, yanked off his boots and left them where they fell. Then he opened the door into the kitchen.

"Ah, heat." Caitlin sighed as the warmth of the house surrounded her.

Trey urged her ahead of him through the house to the hall bathroom. "Strip out of those wet clothes and get into the shower," he ordered. "I'll find something dry for you to put on while your stuff is in the dryer."

Caitlin couldn't imagine what clothing of his would fit her since he was so much bigger, but she was too cold to argue with him. She closed the door and stripped off her wet sweater, jeans, bra and panties, dropping them in a damp pile near the door before she turned on the shower. As hot as she could stand it, the water poured over her chilled body until the heat chased away the goose bumps on her skin and the cold that penetrated her muscles. Warm at last, she turned off the spray and pushed open the shower door, pulling a thick towel from the rail to blot the water from her face. She emerged from the blue terry cloth and froze, staring at the stack of men's clothing on the sink. Her clothes were gone, a damp spot on the shiny linoleum the only evidence that she'd dropped them there.

Trey was here while I was in the shower.

She stepped onto the rug and closed the shower door, staring at it, wondering just how clearly he'd seen her through the smoke-colored glass.

Not too clearly, she decided hopefully.

She toweled herself dry and rummaged below the counter to find a hair dryer, then she ran a comb through the thick tangle of her hair to smooth the strands into their usual neatness before she inspected the clothing Trey had left.

The long-sleeved blue flannel shirt was soft against her skin, the hem reaching nearly to her knees. The sleeves hung far below her fingertips, and she rolled the cuffs up until the flannel reached the middle of her forearm.

The gray sweatpants were warm enough, but the legs were so long they pooled at her ankles. She pulled the waistband up beneath her breasts, but the legs were still too long, and no matter how snug she pulled the tie at the waist, the pants refused to stay up.

"Well, rats." Frustrated, she finally gave up and kicked off the sweatpants, folded them and set them on the counter before she assessed her reflection in the full-length mirror mounted on the door. The hem of Trey's shirt hung nearly to her knees, the shoulder seams were halfway to her elbows, and the top button fastened just below the hollow between her collarbones. "I've worn dresses that showed more skin than this," she decided. "Although I've never been naked under one of them."

But underwear wasn't an option, since her damp bra and panties had disappeared with her jeans and sweater. Satisfied that she was at least decently covered by the soft flannel, she picked up the pair of men's wool socks and headed for the kitchen. Wearing only a pair of faded jeans, Trey stood with his back to the doorway, stirring something in a pan on the stove.

"Hi."

He glanced over his shoulder. "Hi." His glance flicked from the crown of her head to her feet. "What happened to the sweatpants?"

"They were too big. I couldn't keep them up so I left them in the bathroom."

"And the socks?"

She walked toward him, lifting her hand and waggling the wool socks as she leaned against the counter beside him. "Right here. What are you making?"

"Hot chocolate." He moved the pan to the back of the stove and turned off the burner before he took the socks from her. "These will keep you warmer if you actually put them on your feet."

"No kidding. What a revelation! Did you work that out all by yourself?"

"Smart mouth," he said mildly. He tossed the

socks on the counter, then he closed his hands on her waist and lifted her to the countertop.

"Hey," she protested. "Picking me up is getting to be a habit with you. What are you doing now?"

"Making sure that your socks get on your feet." He picked up one foot and frowned at her. "They're cold on the bottom—you should have put the socks on before you left the bathroom."

"The bathroom floor was damp from my wet clothes, and I hate wearing socks with wet spots."

Trey tugged a blue wool sock above her toes and smoothed it over her heel and calf, then repeated the moves with the second sock and foot. "Yeah, well, you wouldn't have had to worry about anything getting wet if I hadn't rolled you in the snow."

"It wasn't your fault that I was standing in the wrong spot when the light bracket decided to dump snow on me."

"No, but it was my fault that you got wet a second time in the snowbank."

"Yes," she said judiciously. "*That* was your fault."

He lifted his head to apologize again, but the teasing twinkle in her green eyes stopped him. "Of course," he said meaningfully, "I wouldn't have rubbed snow in your face if you hadn't shoved a handful of the wet stuff down my jacket first."

"Hmm." Caitlin pretended to consider his claim. "You may be right. I'm not conceding that you are, mind you, but there is a possibility that you have a point." He squeezed her foot threateningly, and she gave in. ''Okay, you do have a point.'' She grinned ruefully at him. ''Actually, I think maybe we're both crazy.''

''Yeah, but it was fun.'' A half smile lifted the corners of his hard mouth. His gaze was soft. ''I haven't had this much fun since the last time you pushed me into a snowbank when you were about thirteen.''

''Have you noticed that we have this odd effect on each other?'' Caitlin asked reflectively.

''Which odd effect? I've noticed more than one.''

She shook her head at him, reproving. ''I'm referring to the fact that we tend to act like a couple of teenagers when we're together.''

''Yeah.'' He tucked a strand of black silk behind her ear, his fingers gentle. ''I think that's a good thing. You make me laugh. I have fun when I'm with you—when I'm not lusting after you, that is.''

''I think I lusted after you when I was thirteen and pushed you into that snowbank,'' Caitlin confessed with a smile.

''Really?'' His eyes lit with interest. ''Too bad I wasn't thirteen, too. We could have necked in the snow. But I must have been...how old? I'm eight years older than you, so that would have made me twenty-one. Nope, I would have been arrested for lusting after a thirteen-year-old.''

''When did you start lusting after me?''

''When you were sixteen and I kissed you under the mistletoe at that Christmas party,'' he said promptly.

''You sound so sure.'' She was seated on the

counter, so her eyes were level with his. His gaze flicked from her eyes to her mouth and lingered, heat flickering to life in the blue depths. His fingers tightened on her leg, his thumb moving in small circles over the smooth, bare skin of her calf above the wool sock.

"I am sure." His voice was husky with growing need. "Absolutely positive." His hand slipped up her calf and found the sensitive skin on the back of her knee. "And I've wanted you ever since."

Caitlin shivered and caught his wrist. "Don't," she whispered, her pulse pounding thickly in time with the stroke of his thumb against her skin.

"Why not?"

"I know you too well, Trey. If we make love, you'll assume that I've agreed to marry you."

His thumb stilled, and he stared at her silently, considering her words for a long moment. "No," he said slowly, shaking his head. "I wouldn't. I won't lie to you," he said bluntly. "I want you to marry me and I'll use anything I can to persuade you. If making love convinces you to be my wife, I won't be sorry, but the plain, unvarnished truth is, I want you. And you want me, too." He cupped her breast and brushed his thumb over the swollen tip that peaked the soft flannel. "Don't you?"

His blunt honesty demanded the same from her. "Yes. I do."

"Then ask me, Caitlin." His voice rasped, thick with hunger. "I won't assume anything except that you want me as much as I want you. I gave you my word. You'll still have all the time you want to make up your mind about marriage. But while you're deciding, neither of us will go to sleep at night frustrated and empty."

His argument was powerfully persuasive. He'd been perfectly clear that he welcomed anything that might convince her to marry him, but in the same breath, he had sworn not to use their lovemaking to pressure her into a decision. Caitlin had never known him to break a promise, even though the keeping of one might have cost him personally.

Trey waited, his hand cupping the weight of her breast, the fingers of his other hand curled possessively around her knee. His gaze met hers without wavering, his body tense and still as he waited for her answer.

His honesty and refusal to seduce her into agreeing was compellingly convincing. Caitlin released his wrist and put her palms on his chest. The sleek, powerful muscles jumped under her touch, and she slid her hands slowly upward to close over his shoulders. She leaned forward, her lips a fraction of an inch from his.

"I want you, Trey. Make love to me. I'm asking," she whispered, slipping her arms around his neck and her fingers into the thick silk of his hair.

He groaned, muttering something unintelligible that was halfway between a curse and a prayer of thanks before his mouth found hers and he shifted her knee slightly so he could step between her thighs. His palm stroked over the smooth skin of her thigh and hip, bare beneath the flannel shirt, before he wrapped his arms around her waist and pulled her close.

Caitlin lost the ability to think. His lips moved from the underside of her jaw down the curve of her throat, his mouth open and hungry, tasting her. Stopped by the shirt collar, he flicked the buttons free and pushed the soft flannel off one shoulder, his open mouth following the gaping cotton over her collarbone to the curve of her shoulder and back to her throat to find the pulse that pounded wildly at the base.

"Wrap your legs around my waist," he repeated. One hand smoothed from upper thigh to knee before cupping her calf and urging her forward.

She obeyed, the worn denim of his jeans faintly abrasive against her calves and heels, the sleek skin of his waist and back furnace hot against her knees and inner thighs. He pressed into her, only the fabric of the soft flannel shirt separating her from him. His mouth closed over the tip of her breast, and Caitlin cried out, a soft, shocked sound. The stroke of his tongue over her swollen, sensitive nipple combined with the wet heat of his mouth as he drew on her sent rivers of heat through her veins. She shuddered, blind with pleasure and arousal. Her fingers flexed convulsively, pressing him closer.

Trey couldn't wait to get her to the bedroom. He ripped open the buttons of his jeans and shoved the edges of the shirt aside. She was hot, wet, swollen, her body welcoming the urgent press of his. He clenched his teeth and eased inside her. She was small, the delicate feminine tissues that surrounded him clinging in soft protest, and he stopped, his whole body taut as he waited for her to adjust, stretching to accommodate him before he flexed his hips and pushed farther inside her. At last, he was buried to the hilt, her legs locked around his waist.

"Trey." Her voice was throaty, slurred with passion.

"You're mine." His voice was guttural, almost indecipherable.

"And you're mine."

His mouth took hers in a deep, wet kiss and his hips flexed, driving into her.

It didn't last nearly long enough. Too much time had passed since they'd been together, and Caitlin quickly exploded, her cries sending Trey tumbling over the edge. Exhausted, boneless, she slumped against the support of his body. Trey dropped his head to her shoulder, sucking in great drafts of air while he held her.

"Damn, that was good," he said fervently when he could finally speak. "Why the hell did you keep saying no for so long?"

"I don't know." She smiled, her lips curving against the sleek skin of his shoulder. "Temporary insanity?"

"Must have been. No sane person would ever say no to this."

"Mmm."

"Put your arms around my neck." He shifted her closer, her face tucked against his throat, then he picked her up and left the kitchen for the hallway.

Trey was still buried inside her, and each step he took stroked him against her. Caitlin kissed his throat and found the soft, warm spot just below his ear. He groaned and swelled with returning arousal, and her lips curved in a small, satisfied smile.

"You're enjoying torturing me, aren't you?" He reached the bedroom and pulled back the spread on the bed. He set her on her feet, the temporary separation agony, before he stripped the shirt from her shoulders and pushed his jeans down his legs, then kicked them aside. "Now it's my turn." He wrapped his arms around her and dropped backward onto the bed.

Caitlin spent the next weeks in a daze of sensual satisfaction. True to his word, Trey didn't use their lovemaking to pressure her into marrying him. Instead, he made love to her with an intensity that left her shaking, sated and eager for the next time. They spent more and more of each day together, but it wasn't until they'd finished dinner one evening several weeks later that Trey mentioned marriage "So, is there going to be a wedding or not?"

"I don't know." Caitlin took two stemmed glasses from the cupboard and glanced sideways at Trey. "Yet."

"Women," Trey said without heat. He opened the carton of milk and filled the glasses Caitlin held in front of him, a teasing half grin lifting his mouth. "Somehow, white milk just isn't the same as white wine. I hope Junior appreciates our abstinence." He opened the refrigerator door, returned the carton to the shelf and followed her into the living room. She was curled on the sofa, her feet tucked beneath her, and he dropped beside her and took the glass she held out.

"Well," he prompted, slipping an arm around her shoulder to tug her nearer. "What's the problem? Why don't you say yes?"

"You freeze me out."

"I freeze you out?" Trey tilted his head and looked at her. "Honey, the last thing in the world I am is cold to you. A constant hot simmer with frequent boiling comes closer to describing how I am when I'm with you."

"I don't mean in bed, Trey. I mean in life." She looked at him, meeting blue eyes that held genuine confusion. She sighed heavily and laid a hand on his thigh. "You don't even know that you do it, do you?"

"Do what?"

"Freeze people out—close yourself off when you decide someone is getting too close."

Trey was silent. During his childhood, he'd developed the ability to mentally step back and isolate himself from people and his surroundings. It was a defense mechanism he'd perfected and used often. He was surprised that Caitlin was aware he did it on occasion. "I don't do that with you," he said quietly, not denying the truth of her words.

"You didn't push me away when I was a little girl," she said gently. "Or maybe I refused to let you get away with it then, and you indulged me. But our relationship changed the summer we became lovers.''

''Of course our relationship changed,'' he agreed. ''You weren't a child anymore. You were a woman, and I was a man who wanted you. Being sexually intimate changed forever the way we see each other.''

''But it didn't have to cause you to throw up walls and shut me out of your life, Trey. Why did it?''

He shifted uneasily, his thumb tracing a slow pattern over the soft skin of her hand against his thigh. ''If you mean when I left to return to duty, I lied to you, Caitlin.''

Caitlin stiffened. ''You lied to me? About what?''

''About that summer meaning no more than a way to spend my furlough having great sex.'' His gaze met hers. ''It meant more, a lot more. But I couldn't ask you to stay with me. My next assignment was in Hong Kong. You had a full scholarship to the University of Washington. If you'd gone with me, you would have had to give up college, and for what? To follow me around from one military post to another for the next four years instead of earning a degree and establishing a career? I couldn't do that to you, so I lied. If you felt that I shut you out and that I was cold to you, I'm sorry, but I had to convince you that the lie was real.''

''That's not exactly what I was referring to, Trey, but since you brought it up, why didn't you tell me how you felt?''

''Because I knew you'd insist on going with me.''

''Maybe I would have,'' she agreed. ''But we'll

never know, will we? Because you didn't respect me enough to let the decision be one that we made together."

"You were only eighteen, Caitlin. I was twenty-six."

"What difference does age make? You're still eight years older than I am. What happens if I marry you and you decide in a few years that I'd be better off without you? What happens then?"

"That wouldn't happen. There's a big difference between an eighteen-year-old girl and a twenty-eight year-old woman."

"Not when it comes to a broken heart. It hurts just as badly at eighteen. Granted, there's got to be a huge difference between dating steadily and actually marrying and living with the man you love. The attachment has to be magnified a thousandfold if you're married. But heartbreak is heartbreak. Only the next time, we'd have a child whose heart would also be broken."

"You think I'd leave you if we were married?"

"I think that as long as you continue to seal your emotions away at will and don't let me into your heart, then you remain solitary and alone. Until you open up and accept me, trust me as a woman you're willing to share your life with, then there are no guarantees about what you may or may not do tomorrow. No matter what you say today."

"You're saying I'm lying to you," he said flatly.

"No. I'm saying you're not willing to share control of your life, of our life, with anyone else. You don't trust anyone but yourself. I don't think you ever have."

"Hell." He plowed his fingers through his hair. "You're wrong. I trust a lot of people."

"Name one."

"Lucas. Josh. Jennifer and Sarah. Zach and CeCe. My C.O. in Colombia. I could go on and on."

"That's not the same as trusting a woman with your heart. It's not the same as trusting a woman enough to admit that you love her."

"We're back to that." He sighed. "I don't believe in love, Caitlin. I won't lie to you and tell you I do."

"I know." She sighed, too, and leaned forward to brush his mouth with a soft kiss before she rose. "It's late, and I really need to get home. I promised Janice that I'd help out at the office tomorrow."

Trey didn't argue. Instead, he drove her home, and when they said good-night at her door, his kiss was fiercely passionate. Although Caitlin kissed him with her usual urgent heat, Trey couldn't rid himself of the uneasy feeling that she was slipping further away from him.

Caitlin lay awake for a long time, staring at the dark ceiling of her bedroom, wondering if Trey would ever understand what she needed from him, unconvinced that she would ever hear him tell her he loved her.

Maybe I'm being unreasonable, she thought. *It's not as if I don't know that he really cares for me, or that he'll be a wonderful father.* But she recognized on a very visceral level that if she didn't destroy the barriers Trey kept between them before they were married, she would lose her opportunity and he would always keep her at arm's length. And she wanted more from him. Much more. She wanted the trust and contentment she'd seen between Josh and Sarah. She needed it just as much as she needed him.

It was far past midnight before she fell asleep, her mind weary with searching for answers.

Chapter Nine

She was tired the next day when Josh found her in the barn, brushing his new mare's already glossy coat.

"Hey." He leaned his forearms on the top rail of the box stall and hooked the heel of one boot over the bottom rail.

"Hey, yourself." Caitlin smiled at him over the mare's back. "What's up?"

"Not much." Josh pushed his hat back on his head and eyed her. "You look like hell," he said bluntly. "Are you still getting sick in the morning?"

"No. I've stopped losing my breakfast before I even eat it," she said. "But thanks for the compliment. I'm delighted to hear that I look ravishing today."

"Oh, hell." He grinned at her. "I didn't say you didn't look ravishing. I said—"

"That I look like hell. Yes, I heard you." She shot him a threatening glare and earned a quick grin and shrug. "You're impossible," she said with a shake of her head. "I don't know how Sarah puts up with you."

"Yeah. It's a mystery," he agreed. He watched her rhythmic strokes of the brush over the horse's back for a few moments. "So, am I going to get to walk you down the aisle?"

"Oh, Uncle Josh." Caitlin sighed with exasperation. "Not you, too."

"Me, too?" He lifted an eyebrow. "Who else wants to walk you down the aisle and give you away?"

"Nobody—at least, not the walking down the aisle part. But everybody keeps asking me when Trey and I are getting married. Sometimes subtly, sometimes not."

"And what's your answer?"

"The same as always. I haven't decided yet."

"Are you planning on deciding sometime in the near future?" he said dryly. "Like, maybe before the kid enters college? Or better yet, before he's born?"

"I hope so." All teasing and exasperation were gone from her voice.

"Is there anything I can do to help?" His deep voice was gentle, concerned.

"I don't think there's anything anyone can do to help. This is up to Trey." She continued to move the brush over the mare's glossy coat in absentminded strokes. ''And I'm not sure he'll ever trust me enough for a marriage between us to work.''

''Is that what this is about—Trey not trusting you?''

She nodded. ''I think that's the core issue. That, and Trey doesn't believe in love.'' She looked at Josh, anguish filling her eyes. ''How can I marry him if he won't love me, Josh?''

''I don't know, sweetheart.'' Josh sighed heavily. ''But I suspect that those two issues are one and the same. He doesn't trust women, therefore he won't let himself love. Or at least he won't admit that he does.''

''But why? I've never hurt him, and he's got to know that I never would, certainly not purposely. Why does he shut me out?''

''If I had to guess, I'd say it's not just you, Caitlin. I think he'd close himself off from any woman he cared about deeply.'' His gaze moved away from her, and he focused on threading a piece of straw between his fingers for a moment while he considered his next words. ''How much do you know about Trey's life before he came to live with us?''

''Not a lot,'' Caitlin admitted. ''I know that his father died before he was born and that he lived with his mother until he was a teenager. Then he came to live with you and Lucas. And I know that his mother drank too much and that Trey doesn't like to talk about her.''

''He *won't* talk about her,'' Josh corrected. ''Trey was fifteen when he came to work for us one summer.

Jennifer was his teacher, and she knew he was headed for trouble, so she talked Lucas into hiring him.'' Josh shook his head, remembering. ''He was one tough kid, but he was willing to work and he was grateful for a roof over his head and food in his belly. He'd pretty much raised himself. His mother fell into a bottle after his father died, and half the time she forgot she had a kid, let alone took care of him. Before the summer was over, Annabel convinced Suzie Weber to go into treatment, and Trey stayed on with us. We all thought we were going to see a happy ending—Suzie would get her act together, settle down and make a life for herself and Trey. But it didn't turn out that way.''

He fell silent, staring unseeingly at the piece of straw.

''Why not? What happened?'' Caitlin prompted, her heart aching for Trey.

''She was sober for two weeks after she was released from the center. Then she disappeared for a few days before she came to the ranch drunk, demanding that Trey go with her, accusing Lucas and Jennifer—and me—of lying to her son and keeping him from her.''

''Did Trey go with her?''

''No. I'll never forget the look on his face. At fifteen, he was already older than his years, but that day he stopped being a kid forever.''

''What did he do?'' Caitlin whispered, heartsick.

''He was cold as ice. Looked at her and told her it didn't matter if Lucas told him that he had to leave with her, he wasn't going. He was never living with her again. Then he turned his back and walked away.'' Josh's gaze met hers. ''As far as I know, he's never seen her since.''

''Oh, Josh.'' Something damp plopped on her hand. She rubbed it away, but another joined it, and she realized she was crying, the tears coursing silently down her cheeks to fall in soft, salty drops against the backs of her fingers.

''Suzie went in and out of treatment more than once, but I understand she's been sober for the last ten years. I don't know if she's tried to see Trey recently. I do know that after that first time, she'd try to contact him each time she finished treatment and was doing well, but he refused to see her. While he was still in high school, she showed up at the ranch a couple of times looking for him, but he knew she was back in town and each time he disappeared before she got here.''

''What happened to her?''

''I heard she finally married and moved to Billings.''

Caitlin knew enough about abused children to make an educated guess about the damage his mother's life-style had done to Trey. She did a quick mental calculation.

''It's been more than twenty years since he's seen her?''

''As far as I know,'' Josh confirmed. ''At least he's never mentioned it, but then, he never mentions his mother at all.''

"Never?"

"Never."

"He told me that he doesn't believe in love because of his mother," Caitlin said slowly, remembering Trey's words and why he didn't believe in love.

"Then you're probably the only one of us he's talked to about her in all this time." His gaze pinned her. "That must mean something, Caitlin."

"Maybe." She sighed deeply. "But that doesn't solve the problem. It sounds to me as if Trey is holding every woman accountable for his mother's actions, refusing to trust anyone because his mother betrayed him. That's not fair."

"No," Josh agreed. "That's not fair. But he's a grown man, Caitlin. I don't know how you go back and fix what happened all those years ago. Do you?"

"No, I don't." Tears welled again. "Maybe it's hopeless."

"No." Josh pulled open the gate and held out a hand. "It's not hopeless. Not when a woman loves a man as much as you love Trey. You do love him, don't you?"

"Oh, yes. Since I was twelve years old. It just doesn't seem to go away."

"Then it will work out. Come on, put that brush away and let's get something hot to drink. This barn is too damn cold."

"All right." Caitlin took his hand and let him pull her into the aisle.

He slung an arm over her shoulders and gave her

a quick, hard hug. ''Hang in there, Caitlin. You two love each other, and this will work out.''

''Mmm.'' Caitlin was immeasurably warmed by Josh's support, but she wasn't at all sure she was convinced the problems with Trey would work themselves out. Not without a genuine miracle.

The house was a small, one-story ranch located on a quiet residential street on the outskirts of Billings.

Caitlin set the parking brake and peered out the windshield, double-checking the address on the house with the note in her hand.

This is it. Suzie Weber, now Andersen, had been cautiously welcoming when Caitlin telephoned, introduced herself and requested to meet with her about Trey.

Caitlin stepped out of the car and started up the sidewalk, hoping fervently for her miracle. She barely touched the doorbell when the door opened, revealing a small, blond woman dressed in a conservative blue silk blouse and slacks.

''Good morning. You must be Caitlin.''

''Yes, yes, I am. And you're Mrs. Andersen?''

''Yes.'' The woman stepped back, still holding fast to the door. ''Won't you come in?''

''Thank you.'' Caitlin stepped into the entryway.

''Let me take your coat.''

Caitlin slipped out of her wool coat and hesitated while Mrs. Andersen found a wooden hanger and tucked it away in the hall closet.

"Let's go into the living room."

Caitlin found a seat on the sofa, and Suzie Andersen perched nervously on the edge of a cushioned armchair facing her.

"I suppose you're wondering why I wanted to speak with you," Caitlin began.

"You wanted to talk to me about Trey." The older woman hesitated and paused to draw a deep, steadying breath. "Are you married to Trey?"

"No. We're not married, not yet," Caitlin responded. "But we may be, in the near future."

"Ah. I see."

But Caitlin could read the confusion in the older woman's polite expression and knew that Trey's mother was wondering what she wanted from her. Suzie Andersen was also clearly nervous, her fingers moving over the fringe of the tasseled pillow beside her on the chair.

"Whether or not we marry may depend on you."

"On me?" Mrs. Andersen's fingers froze, clutching the soft pillow.

"Yes. Mrs. Andersen, how long has it been since you've seen Trey or talked to him?"

"Nearly twenty years." The woman's voice trembled, and she caught her breath.

"Was that Trey's choice or yours?"

This time there was no disguising the sob that Trey's mother stifled before she could speak. "It...it was Trey's decision." She lifted her chin, tears hovering as she said firmly, "And I don't fault him for it. He had the right to choose. I'm sure you know why. If you're thinking of marrying, he must have told you about his childhood.''

''Very little, Mrs. Andersen. In fact, I'm told he rarely, if ever, discusses you or his childhood with anyone.''

Suzie Andersen flinched as if she'd taken a body blow. ''I didn't know,'' she said, shaken. ''I'd hoped...I've always assumed that he'd gone to counseling, maybe joined a group for adult children of—'' She broke off and abruptly looked away. She brushed trembling fingers across her cheeks, sweeping away tears, then she straightened, her back ramrod straight. She folded her hands in her lap, her gaze returning to Caitlin. ''I've kept track of Trey through the years by keeping in touch with friends and acquaintances who live in Butte Creek. I assume that gossip would make you aware of at least some of Trey's background, but if you're thinking of marrying him, you deserve to know what I can tell you.'' Again she paused. ''I'm an alcoholic. I have been since a year or so after Trey was born. Children need adults to take care of them, but all Trey had was a child who couldn't take care of herself, let alone a one-year-old. When he was fifteen, Lucas Hightower hired him for summer labor. I was faced with losing my son forever, and the possibility gave me the incentive needed to enter inpatient treatment. Unfortunately—'' she glanced at Caitlin, her face anguished ''—I relapsed within a few weeks after I was released. Trey's never forgiven me, and he's refused to see or speak to me ever since.''

''Do you know why?'' Caitlin asked gently.

"He cut me out of his life and moved on," Suzie said bleakly. "And I don't blame him. He couldn't have had a worse mother. And he found a new family with the Hightowers. He no longer needs me."

"I don't think that's true, Mrs. Andersen," Caitlin said gently. "I think Trey cares very much for Lucas and Jennifer and Josh and Sarah, but I think he also needs to resolve those long-ago issues with you before he can truly move on."

"What makes you think so?" Suzie's thin body tensed. "Is something wrong? Isn't he happy?"

Worry lined the older woman's face, and her blue eyes were anxious.

"He isn't unhappy," Caitlin said slowly, choosing her words carefully. "But he wants us to marry, and I think he needs to speak with you to discuss any unresolved issues that may remain."

Trey's mother shook her head in confusion. "Unresolved issues? I'm not sure what those may be, but I'm more than willing to do anything that Trey wants of me to make up for the years I failed so miserably at being a parent. His only parent," she added bleakly. "Does he want me to go to counseling with him? Does he want to speak to me, see me?" she asked hopefully.

Caitlin hated to extinguish the woman's spark of hope. "Trey doesn't know that I came here today, Mrs. Andersen. I'm not sure how he'll react when I tell him I've spoken with you."

Suzie seemed to shrink in the cushioned chair. "I see," she said quietly.

''But I think it's important that he speak with you, meet with you face-to-face.'' Caitlin leaned forward. ''I'm so pleased that you're willing to see him.''

Tears flowed unchecked down Suzie's cheeks. ''He's my son. I love him,'' she said simply. ''Just because I was a bad parent doesn't mean that I've ever stopped loving him and hoping that someday he could find it in his heart to forgive me.''

Trey looked up at the sound of a car engine, leaving the bread half-buttered on the counter along with the ham and cheese for his lunch, to peer out the window. Caitlin's little red car was parked outside his front gate. He left the kitchen, strode to the front door and yanked it open.

''Hi,'' he called. She looked over her shoulder and smiled, latching the gate before she turned and moved up the sidewalk. He met her at the top of the porch steps and wrapped his arms around her, lifting her off her feet. He kissed the tip of her nose, her cheeks and temples as he moved into the house. He kicked the door shut and pinned her against it at the same time his mouth covered hers.

''You've got too many clothes on,'' he muttered, tugging the buttons open on her coat and unwrapping the red wool muffler before shoving them off her shoulders. Coat and muffler fell in a heap at her feet, and his lips found her throat. ''That's better,'' he said.

''Trey. Trey?'' Caitlin gasped and caught her breath as his hands moved under her sweater. ''What are you doing?''

He went still.

"You can't tell?" He lifted his head, his eyes hot. "I must be doing something wrong."

"No," she said, her voice throaty. "You're definitely not doing anything wrong."

"Good." He dropped his head, and his tongue found the pulse at the base of her throat.

"But it's barely lunchtime, and I need to talk to you."

"We'll talk. After. And I know it's lunchtime. I'm hungry, starving...." He slipped the button free at her waistband and slid the zipper down, his hand unerringly finding her center. "Ah, sweetheart," he breathed. "What did I ever do to deserve you?"

His fingers began a lingering caress before he swung her into his arms and carried her to the bedroom. He set her on her feet next to the bed, grabbed the bottom of her green sweater and with one swift pull peeled it off over her head. She emerged with rumpled black hair and a faintly bemused expression. Trey unhooked her bra, nudged her backward on the bed and efficiently stripped her first of her boots and then her jeans, leaving her clad only in the loosened pink bra and matching lace bikini panties.

Caitlin lay on the bed and watched him rip off his flannel shirt and tug off boots and jeans. She barely had time to register the impact of sleek, honed muscles before he was stretched out beside her.

"Pretty as these are, honey, I think they have to come off." He slipped the bra straps from her shoulders and slid the bikini down her legs, tossing them over his shoulder without looking away from her. He smoothed his palm over the swell of her breast, brushing the thrust of her nipple with his callused thumb. "Are you still tender?" he murmured, his gaze searching her face for any evidence of discomfort.

"Yes, but that doesn't hurt."

"Tell me if it does." His voice was raspy, thick with the effort it took to speak. Then he slipped an arm under her and covered the tip of her breast with his mouth.

Caitlin gasped and closed her eyes, her cheek finding the silky crown of his head. The suction of his mouth against her breast pounded through her veins, heat pulsing hotter and hotter. His hand brushed the apex of her thighs, lingering to stroke the satiny skin of her inner thighs and the softer curls between before finding the hot, liquid center of her. She twisted in his grasp, arching against the heated torment of his hands and mouth.

"Please," she begged. "Trey..."

He pulled her thigh over his and found her, pushing against her wet heat with insistent force. She shuddered as he stretched her, mindless with the nearly unbearable pleasure of having him inside her, frantic with the need to have all of him. With one last thrust he was home, seated deep, and she wrapped her legs around his waist, holding him while her inner muscles flexed, rippling around the thick, heavy length of him.

"Don't move." He ground the words out, his voice guttural. Her muscles convulsed again, and he swore, unable to keep from moving as her sheath squeezed and stroked him. His hips flexed, hers answered, and he lost all control.

Neither Caitlin nor Trey knew whose hunger fed whom. Hot strokes and pleasured groans filled the silence until Caitlin screamed with release and Trey swiftly followed her over the edge.

Caitlin was too drained to move. Eyes closed, her lips curved in a smile as Trey's finger traced her mouth.

"Good?" he asked.

"Mmm. Good," she answered.

He shifted, lying spread-eagled on the bed, and groaned. "You're going to kill me, woman."

Caitlin opened one eye and turned her head to look at him, her body still incapable of movement. "*I'm* going to kill *you?* Who attacked whom?"

He rolled his head sideways and grinned at her. "Are you sure that's proper English, Professor?"

"Who cares." She smiled, eyeing his naked body. "I don't care who started this—it was a great idea."

"You're right." He rolled toward her and pulled her on top of him, tucking her head under his chin. "Who cares who attacked who. I love having you naked in my bed."

"Mm," Caitlin agreed sleepily. Her stomach grumbled.

"Uh-oh. That reminds me. I was fixing lunch when you drove in. Are you hungry?"

"I'm starving. All I ate for breakfast was a slice of toast with peanut butter."

"Then I better feed you and Junior."

His palm stroked her waist, smoothing the faint, outward curve of her tummy before lightly swatting her bottom.

"Get up, woman. I need food."

He lifted her off him and stood, then bent to collect his jeans.

Caitlin indulged herself, watching the play of sleek muscles as he stepped into them. He buttoned his jeans and glanced up to catch her eyeing him.

"Come on, lazybones." He leaned his fists against the rumpled blue bedspread on either side of her face and bent to taste her mouth just one more time. "Get up," he said, his voice deeper, huskier than a moment before. "Before I join you and we miss lunch altogether."

He twined his fingers through hers and tugged gently. Caitlin sighed and sat up, catching the flannel shirt he tossed her. She pushed her hands through the sleeves and stood, but before she could button it, Trey did. The backs of his fingers against her sensitized skin as he moved down her body tucking buttons through buttonholes had her shivering with pleasure. His head was bent, his eyes focused on the task. Tousled from her fingers, his blond hair was rumpled. His eyes were heavy-lidded with satisfaction, his lower lip fuller and faintly swollen from kissing her.

"Stop that," he ordered without looking up.

"What?" she whispered.

"You know what." His eyes were blue fire when he finished the last button and his gaze met hers. "First, I feed you." He pressed a hot, quick kiss against her mouth, his tongue licking her lower lip. "Then you feed me. I'm hungry again."

"All right." Caitlin didn't protest when he took her hand and drew her with him to the kitchen.

Caitlin searched for an opening to broach the subject of his mother. But it wasn't until they'd eaten, made love again, showered together and were getting dressed that she found an opportunity.

"I went to Billings yesterday." She pulled on her boots and stood, smoothing her sweater over her waist, instinctively stroking the barely noticeable curve of her tummy.

"Yeah? What did you buy?" Trey stuffed his shirttails into his jeans and buttoned them, then buckled his belt with economical movements.

"Well, actually…nothing."

"Nothing?" He caught her hand, threading his fingers through hers, and tugged her gently after him to the kitchen. He pulled out a stool at the counter and released her, crossing the room to the coffeemaker. "I can't believe that you went shopping and didn't buy any clothes." He poured coffee into mugs and returned to drop onto a stool beside her, handing her a steaming mug. "Decaf," he commented, in answer to the dubious look she gave him. Her brow cleared, and she sipped. "You sure you didn't buy anything? Like maybe another of those lacy teddy things I like so much?"

"No. No lingerie." Caitlin drew a deep breath and let it out slowly. "I had an appointment to meet someone in Billings."

"Really? Who?"

"Your mother."

Trey's head shot up. He didn't sip from the mug at his lips. Instead, he set it on the counter. Jaw hard, eyes narrowed, he stared at her unblinkingly for a long, silent moment.

"Why?"

"I needed to know if your estrangement was her wish or yours."

"And what did you find out?"

"That you choose not to see your mother."

"Why didn't you ask me? I would have told you," he said grimly.

"Because I wanted to meet her and find out if she'd be willing to talk with you."

"Why?"

"Because I think you need to resolve issues with your mother before you can be happy building a life with me."

"My mother doesn't have anything to do with you and me. I haven't seen her since I was a kid. And I don't want to," he said flatly.

Caitlin reached out, covering his hand with hers, but he pulled away, distancing himself. "I want us to be married, to be a family—the two of us and our baby. But you don't trust me. I don't think you trust women in general. I'm not a psychiatrist, Trey, but I think that lack of trust stems from your relationship with your mother."

"You're right," he said bluntly. "You're not a psychiatrist. Leave it be, Caitlin. I don't want to drag up what I settled years ago. There isn't anything I can learn from my mother. And if there were, it wouldn't be good."

"Maybe you can learn what's keeping you from believing in love."

"That's the last thing anybody, including me, could ever learn from Suzie Weber."

"Andersen. Her name is Suzie Andersen now—she's married."

"It's nothing to me what she's done."

He was stubborn, his mind clearly closed. Caitlin struggled to find a way to convince him. "I've told you often enough about the struggles I had with my mother. She won't win any medals for mother of the year, either, but we've come to terms with each other, and with the people we were and the things that happened when I was little. I can't tell you how strongly I feel about the importance of adults confronting their parents and working through problems left over from childhood."

"I accept that you think it's important. You'll have to accept that I don't agree."

"But, Trey, it's not just a personal issue or a personal opinion. Some of the best psychologists and family counselors in the country agree that adults need to come to terms with abuse from their childhood before they can go on to live happy, full lives."

"Well, I don't agree with you, Caitlin. Why can't you accept that? What do you want from me?"

"I want you to be able to say, 'I love you.' I need to hear it, and I think you need to say it."

"Hell. We've had this conversation before. I don't believe in love, and even if I did, I don't think I'm capable of loving anyone. So I'm never going to lie and say, 'I love you.'"

"You're ducking this, Trey. Refusing to deal with your mother is a coward's way out."

"I'm no coward," he snarled, insulted. "I've faced death more times than I can count, been wounded and went back into battle. I'm not a coward."

"That's physical danger. I've no doubt that you'd walk through hell and never flinch. I'm talking about emotional danger. You won't face your mother and deal with the hurt she caused you all those years ago. You turned your back on her twenty years ago, and you've been running ever since. You're afraid to love, afraid that if you commit to loving someone, you'll be vulnerable and hurt again."

The words struck home, cutting straight to the heart of the fears he'd hidden since he was a child. Inside, Trey bled. Outside, he was stone-faced and still.

"Maybe it's a good thing that we had this conversation." His voice was as cold and expressionless as his face. "If that's your opinion of my character, perhaps it's best that we don't marry. We'd be doomed before we started."

"Perhaps you're right." Pale and sick with loss, Caitlin left the kitchen on trembling legs. Numbly, she found her coat and left the house. It wasn't until she turned onto the highway that she realized she was crying, deep, racking sobs that shook her body.

She'd gambled and lost. Trey would never let her into his heart.

Trey stood where she left him. He heard the front door close, heard the low grumble of her car engine as it turned over, heard the tires crunch over snow and the fading of engine noise until at last there were no more sounds. He was alone. Caitlin was gone. This time for good.

He threw the mug and it shattered, coffee spraying against the wall.

"Woof!" Chukka barked, raced into the room and halted.

"Never mind, Chukka." Trey strode across the room, snapped his fingers at the Lab to follow and grabbed his jacket and hat from the rack by the door. "Women," he growled. "They always have to try to fix things. Well, I don't want her fixing things. Things are just fine the way they are."

He worked for hours shoveling snow, and when dusk turned swiftly into full dark, he moved into the barn and stacked hay bales.

Finally, muscles screaming in protest, he dragged himself to the house and took a shower. Then he located a nearly full bottle of medicinal whiskey in the back of a cabinet and proceeded to get drunk. The next morning, he woke with a rolling stomach and a screaming headache. He took aspirin and slugged down a quart of coffee. Then he grimly went back to work. No job was too difficult, too dirty, too unnecessary for him to tackle. He polished tack that already gleamed and decided to move hay bales again.

He was miserable. No amount of physical labor eased the pain in his heart. No amount of denying drove away the fear that Caitlin might be right.

Chapter Ten

His temper hadn't improved any three days later when the sound of a car engine interrupted the noon silence.

Caitlin?

He left his sandwich half made on the kitchen counter and yanked back the curtain to look out the window.

It wasn't Caitlin. Sarah Hightower pulled open the gate and started up the sidewalk, Analisa beside her.

"Damn," he muttered. Unable to quell a surge of disappointment, he left the kitchen to pull open the front door. "Hello, Sarah. Analisa. What brings you two out?" He watched Sarah's eyes widen and darken with concern as her gaze flickered over him. It occurred to him that he hadn't shaved in three days, and the bathroom mirror had told him this morning that he looked like hell. Evidently, Sarah thought so, too.

''Hello, Trey.'' She glanced at the little girl by her side. ''Analisa insisted that she needed to talk to you about something very important. Do you have a few minutes to talk to her?''

Trey looked at the girl. Her face was solemn, her chin determined, her brown eyes unreadable as she met his gaze. He was in no mood for company, but the kid clearly had something on her mind. He sighed silently and opened the door wide.

''Sure. Come on in.'' Analisa followed Sarah into the house. Trey closed the door behind them and led them into the kitchen. ''I was just making lunch. Are you hungry?''

''No, thank you. Do you have any coffee?'' Sarah asked. At Trey's nod, she crossed to the cupboard and with the ease of familiarity took out a mug and filled it. ''Analisa wants to speak to you alone, so I'll wait in the living room.'' Cup in hand, she crossed the room and disappeared.

Puzzled, Trey looked from the empty doorway to the little girl. She was watching him intently. He shoved the fingers of one hand through his hair and raked it off his forehead.

''Have a seat, Analisa.''

She perched on a stool at the counter, tucked the toes of her tennis shoes over a rung and continued to eye him silently.

Trey filled his mug and opened the cupboard, found the aspirin bottle and shook out three tablets. He downed them with a swig of hot coffee, grimaced and turned to face the little girl.

"Okay, kid, shoot. What's up?"

"Caitlin's sad. And her eyes are red, so I'm sure she's been crying," Analisa said bluntly. "She's been that way since she came home from your house the other day. What did you say to her?"

Trey sipped his coffee, reined in his bad temper and reminded himself that she was just a little girl. "What makes you think she's sad because of something I said?"

"Because I heard her tell Aunt Sarah that there isn't going to be a wedding. And then I heard her crying after I went to bed last night. I could hear her 'cause her bedroom's right next to mine." She glared at him, her small hands clasped into fists in her lap. "I thought you were nice, but you're not."

"I never told you I was nice," Trey growled, glaring at her.

"Well, you're not," she said emphatically. "Why aren't you going to marry Caitlin? I thought you liked her."

"I do like her."

"Then you shouldn't be making her cry."

The kid was stubborn as a mule, and she was making him feel as if she'd caught him pulling wings off butterflies.

"Look, kid, I didn't mean to make her cry. Sometimes adults have arguments."

"You guys had an argument?" Her brown eyes narrowed suspiciously. "Did you yell at her?"

"No. I didn't yell at her." Trey searched for something that would get the kid off his back without telling her the truth. "We didn't agree about something, that's all."

"What?"

"Something she wanted me to do."

"Why didn't you just do it?" Analisa demanded.

"Because I didn't want to," he said tersely.

"Why not?"

"Just because."

"My teacher says that 'just because' isn't a good reason." Analisa frowned at him.

"It's the only one you're going to get."

She crossed her arms. "I don't like it when Caitlin's sad."

Tears hovered on her lashes, then rolled slowly down her cheeks. Her voice quivered with the effort it took to keep it from breaking. Trey could deal with stubborn and demanding, he had no defense against tears.

"Aw, hell. Don't cry." He tore a paper towel from the roll on a spindle under a cabinet and handed it to her. "Here. You're leaking all over my kitchen." She took the towel and mopped her face. Trey knew she was attached to Caitlin. Abandoned by her mother, living with a new family, Analisa was probably hypersensitive to any threats to the stability of her world. And there was no question Caitlin was an important part of her world. She was watching him hopefully, and he sighed heavily. "I didn't mean to make Caitlin sad. I certainly didn't mean to make her cry."

"Couldn't you just do what she wanted you to do, whatever it was, so she won't be sad anymore?"

Trey scrubbed his hand down his face and shook his head. "I don't think so, Analisa."

"Why not? Would you get in trouble for doing it?"

"No."

"Would it hurt you?"

"Yes." The word came out of nowhere, stark and honest. It stunned Trey.

"Oh. Then I guess you can't do it," she said sorrowfully. "Because then you and Caitlin would both be sad."

Not both of us. Trey couldn't avoid the truth. It would make Caitlin happy if he went to see his mother. How much could seeing the woman who gave birth to him hurt? He didn't know. He did know the thought of resurrecting dark memories caused a cold lump in his stomach. He'd taken great pains during the early years to avoid Suzie Weber. After the first five or six years, however, it was almost a conditioned reflex to leave a room if he heard her name, to leave town if he heard she was visiting Butte Creek. *How much would it hurt?* He didn't know, but maybe he was going to have to find out.

"Tell you what, kid." He took the soft paper towel from Analisa's fingers and dabbed the dampness from her cheeks. "I'll see what I can do to make Caitlin happy again, all right?"

"Really?"

The uncertainty in her eyes told Trey how little she relied on an adult's promise.

"I promise," he said, sketching an X over his chest with his forefinger. "And I never break a promise. Ask Caitlin."

"Okay." The look she gave him was skeptical, but at least the steady stream of tears had stopped. "Will you make her happy soon?"

"Women," Trey muttered. "You're all the same."

Her solemn face wrinkled in confusion. "What women?"

"Never mind." He caught her under the arms and lifted her from the stool. "Go on home with Sarah and stop worrying." She started toward the doorway, and he stopped her with a hand on her arm. "And don't tell Caitlin about this conversation."

"Why?"

"Because I'll tell her myself."

"When?"

"Just as soon as I do what I need to do to make her happy again."

"Okay. But hurry up."

She waited until he nodded before she faced front again and walked ahead of him into the living room. Sarah was seated on the sofa, a magazine spread open on her lap, her empty coffee mug on the floor beside her.

"I'm ready to go home now," Analisa announced, stopping a few feet from her.

"All right." Sarah's shrewd gaze swept over Analisa's damp lashes before meeting Trey's. She lifted an eyebrow in silent inquiry. Trey shrugged without comment.

Ten minutes later, he stood at the window and watched them drive away.

It took two days of soul-searching before Trey picked up the telephone and dialed the number. Someone picked it up on the fourth ring.

"Hello?"

The female voice was softer than he remembered, less strident.

"Hello. Is Mrs. Andersen in?"

"Speaking. Who is this?"

"This is Trey."

He heard his mother's soft gasp.

"Trey." Her voice shook, barely audible.

He focused on the reason for the call and ignored the cold anger that clawed at his stomach and pounded at his temples. "I understand that Caitlin came to see you."

"Yes. Yes, she did."

"She told me that you wouldn't object to seeing me."

"No, of course I wouldn't object." Her voice wavered. She swallowed audibly and took a deep breath before she continued. "I'd very much like to see you."

I don't want to see you, he thought grimly, but he didn't say the words. "I can be in Billings tomorrow morning. Would ten o'clock be a good time?"

"Ten o'clock would be just fine."

"All right. I'll see you then."

"I'm looking forward to it. Goodbye, Trey."

"Goodbye."

Trey hung up the phone and stood staring at it for a long moment, wishing he could call back and cancel, wishing he didn't have to go within a hundred miles of Billings, Montana, knowing that he couldn't back out now.

"One time," he said grimly. "One short visit. Then maybe Caitlin will accept that there aren't any miracles that will turn me and my mother into the Beaver Cleaver family."

Trey forced himself to stride swiftly up the walk to his mother's house the next morning. He rapped his knuckles on the door, and before his hand lowered, the door swung inward.

He barely recognized the woman standing in the doorway.

Gone was the tousled mop of hair that she used to bleach white-blond. Gone, too, were the heavy makeup and cheap perfume. This small woman was a good twenty pounds lighter than the Suzie he remembered, her hair a smooth cap of graying blond, her lined face discreetly made up, her green flowered dress conservative. Only the eyes, as light blue as his, were familiar.

Was this small, vulnerable woman the same female who had given birth to him, then left him to fend for himself while she chased an elusive dream of happiness?

"Trey." She reached for him but stopped short of touching him. "Won't you come in?"

Trey stepped over the threshold, and she closed the door behind them.

Trey knocked on Caitlin's door the next evening. The porch light flicked on, and Josh pulled open the door.

"Evenin', Trey. Come on in."

Trey stamped the snow off his boots and stepped into the entryway. Josh glanced past him at the steadily falling snow and closed the door. "It's still coming down. How are the roads?"

"Not bad," Trey replied. "But it's starting to drift in places."

"I better warn Charlie to make sure the snowplow is ready for tomorrow morning." Josh tucked his hands into his back pockets. "Take your coat off, Trey. You can stay a while, can't you?"

"Actually, I was hoping to talk Caitlin into coming over to my place."

"Hmm. Caitlin!"

"Yes?" She came to the top of the stairs and halted abruptly, her gaze fixed on Trey.

"Trey's here." Josh turned to the younger man. "If you change your mind about staying, come on out in the kitchen. Sarah baked chocolate cake today."

"Thanks, Josh." Trey knew Josh left, but his gaze never left Caitlin. She was paler than the last time he'd seen her, and faint blue circles underlined her eyes. Black leggings covered her legs, and an emerald green sweater reached halfway to her knees, green wool socks on her small feet. She stood at the head of the stairs, one hand on the banister, her eyes dark with emotion.

''Hello, Caitlin.''

''Hi.''

''Will you come with me? I need to talk to you.''

She hesitated, torn between wanting to go with him and knowing that any conversation between them was likely to end painfully.

''Please,'' he said quietly. ''Hear me out. I promise I'll bring you straight home afterward if you want.''

For a long moment she remained silent.

''All right.'' She glanced at her stockinged feet. ''I'll get my shoes and coat.''

She disappeared, and Trey drew a deep breath, relieved that at least she was willing to talk to him. He hadn't been sure that she would agree.

''I'm ready.'' Boots on, warm wool coat buttoned to her chin, she joined Trey at the bottom of the stairs. He held the door open, closed it behind them and took her arm.

Snow drifted down, catching on their shoulders, arms, even Caitlin's eyelashes as she tilted her face to the white flakes. Thick and white, the snowfall was deceptively gentle. Though only a slight wind drove the cold flakes, already there were several inches on the ground.

''I shouldn't stay out long,'' Caitlin commented as

Trey tucked her into the truck cab. "The snow looks like it could close the roads."

"It might," Trey agreed. He slammed the door and rounded the hood of the truck to join her in the warm cab. "I'll have you home before the roads get bad."

They didn't speak again until they were inside Trey's house, their snow-dampened coats hung on hooks to dry.

"Let's go into the kitchen," he said, ushering her ahead of him. He pulled out a chair at the small table and seated her before fetching coffeepot and mugs from the kitchen. "It's decaf," he said, filling their mugs.

"Thank you," she murmured. She cupped the mug, welcoming the heat as she waited for him to speak. Her heart ached, and it was painfully difficult to look at his beloved face. He looked tired, the lines that fanned from the corners of his eyes etched deeper, his mouth somber and unsmiling. She braced herself, expecting him to ask her about financial arrangements or visitation schedules for their child, dreading the necessary conversation but wanting it over with. "What is it you wanted to talk to me about, Trey?"

"I went to see my mother yesterday."

The flat statement caught her unaware, and she could only stare at him, stunned.

"You did what?"

"I talked to my mother yesterday," he repeated. Trey didn't know what Caitlin had expected him to say, but her stunned features told him that his words came as a complete surprise.

"Oh." Caitlin didn't know what to say. Deep inside, a tiny bud of hope began to slowly unfurl. "What did you talk about?"

"You. And me. And her. About our life when we lived together." His gaze left hers, and he stared at the black brew in his cup. "About why she did the things she did. Why she drank, how much she loved my father."

Caitlin tried not to read too much into his words. "Was it as difficult as you thought it would be?" she asked, concerned.

"Yes." He looked at her, a small smile flashing. Just as quickly, it disappeared. "And no. I didn't want to see her, and I never would have if it hadn't been for you. But painful as it was to talk about the bad days, there was something freeing about having her tell me that none of it was my fault. I'm thirty-six years old and never realized that somehow, down deep, I still felt responsible for her drinking."

"Oh, Trey, no." Caitlin covered his hand with hers, and he immediately turned his hand palm up, threading his fingers through hers in a warm clasp.

"That's not uncommon for children of alcoholics," he commented, contemplating the slim fingers bound with his. "She gave me a couple of books. I've only read one of them so far, but apparently I'm not the only one who feels that way." His gaze met hers. "I'm not saying that Suzie and I are friends after all these years, Caitlin, but at least, we're not enemies."

"I'm glad, Trey." Emotion clogged her throat and fogged her vision. She brushed her fingertips across her misty eyes and managed a wavering smile. "I'm so glad."

"Visiting my mother isn't the only thing I wanted to talk to you about," Trey said, his voice husky. His muscles tensed against the need to pull her out of her chair and onto his lap to hold her. He needed her close, tucked against his heart.

He hesitated, his thumb moving in small circles over the back of her hand. Caitlin waited, barely breathing under the intensity of his stare.

"I know you need to hear me say that I love you, Caitlin," he said, his voice as dark as his eyes. "But I still don't know what the word means. I know that without you, I'm lonely, restless and miserable. All the years that we were apart, I grieved for you. It wasn't until that night in Seattle that I felt whole again. Leaving you sleeping in your bed was the hardest thing I've ever done. I felt guilty as hell when I learned you were pregnant, but part of me was glad that the baby gave me an excuse to be a part of your life. No one else makes me laugh the way you do, and making love with you is as close to heaven as a man can get. I can't think of anything better than knowing that we'll raise a child together. I know it's not just lust I feel, Caitlin, but whether it's love or not—" he shrugged helplessly "—I don't know."

"Oh, Trey." Caitlin smiled through the tears that trickled down her cheeks and salted the curve of her lips. "You've just given me the best definition of love any woman could hope for. You do love me."

"Yeah?" Relief flooded Trey. He forced himself

not to grab her. "So." He cleared his throat. "Does that mean you'll marry me? Even if I can't say the words?"

She nodded solemnly. "Yes. Even if you can't say the words."

He shoved back his chair and tugged her out of her seat. "Come here."

She went willingly, her arms slipping around his neck as he pulled her onto his thighs and his mouth found hers.

Epilogue

The strains of the wedding march filled the flower-bedecked church. On each side of the green and gold draped altar, candelabras held tapered candles flanked by huge white wicker baskets of flowers. One step above Trey and Lucas on the red carpet, the minister waited patiently. All three faced the empty aisle and the back of the sanctuary with its closed doors. Trey wasn't nearly as patient as the minister.

In the anteroom, the minister's wife whispered last-minute instructions to the row of cousins, the boys in classic black tuxedos and bow ties, the girls in long bridesmaids' dresses in varying shades of green from pale spring grass to deep emerald. Analisa giggled at a whispered comment from Samantha, and Justin hushed them with a threatening glare.

Josh patted Caitlin's fingers, pale against the black sleeve of his tuxedo.

"Ready?"

"Ready."

Her swift but wobbly smile reassured him, and he nodded at the usher. The double doors opened, and the line of junior bridesmaids and groomsmen moved sedately forward, keeping pace with the organ's stately march.

Caitlin's breath caught, butterflies fluttering nervously in her stomach. She pressed the armful of fragrant hothouse flowers closer and drew in a deep breath, counting slowly as she exhaled. The last junior couple stepped through the doors into the church and started down the aisle. Then Josh led her forward, pausing in the center of the doorway.

The church was packed with family and friends, but familiar faces faded into a blur as she searched for and found Trey. He stood at the end of the red carpet to the right of the minister, waiting. Her gaze locked with his, and instantly the butterflies stopped. The tuxedo fit smoothly across his broad shoulders, the severe black highlighting his blond hair and the stark white of the tucked shirt. He was heart-stoppingly handsome in the formal clothes, but it was the expression in his deep blue eyes that banished her nerves and drew her down the aisle toward him.

She's beautiful, Trey thought. So beautiful in the long white dress that she took his breath away. A gauzy white veil rose from a beaded headpiece on the crown of her head and floated down the back of the dress to brush against the red carpet behind her. The lace-covered and bead-studded bodice was scoop-necked, the narrow, arm-hugging sleeves ending in shallow lacy points just below her wrists. The skirt was full and flowing, billowing against Josh's black tuxedo as they moved slowly down the aisle. She cradled the bouquet he'd sent her, the white lilies and orchids tucked among pink and red roses and tiny blue flowers that Trey didn't recognize, while the emerald green ribbons trailed down the front of her skirts.

He'd dreamed of marrying Caitlin. His dreams hadn't done her justice.

Caitlin and Josh reached the end of the aisle. Josh bent to brush her cheek with a kiss, and she tore her gaze from Trey's to smile a thank-you at her beloved uncle. Then he stepped back to take his seat beside Sarah in the front pew, and Trey took her hand, drawing her forward to face the altar.

The minister began the service. Caitlin struggled to listen to the solemn words but was distracted by the press of Trey's warmth along her side as they knelt at the altar, and the comforting clasp of his hand around hers as they stood to take their vows.

"I, Trey Aaron Weber, take thee, Caitlin Margaret Drummond, to be my wedded wife."

His voice was deep and sure. Tears welled, spilling over to move slowly down her cheeks. Trey slipped the wedding band on her finger and gently wiped the tears from her face with his fingertips.

"Repeat after me," the minister said soothingly. "I, Caitlin Margaret Drummond..."

"I, Caitlin Margaret Drummond," she began, her voice trembling with emotion, then growing stronger as she saw the love written on Trey's face. She finished the vows and slid the heavy gold wedding band on his finger.

"I now pronounce you man and wife. You may kiss the bride."

Trey slipped his arms around her waist and pulled her close, the gesture both claiming and sheltering.

"I love you," he whispered, his heart in his eyes as he looked at her.

"I love you, too," she whispered.

And then his mouth took hers and banished forever any lingering doubts. When he lifted his head and looked at her, she recognized the fierce satisfaction in his eyes. She felt the same way.

A hand on each of their shoulders, the minister gently turned them to face the crowded sanctuary. "Ladies and gentlemen, Mr. and Mrs. Weber."

The pews emptied as the audience stood, clapping, cheering and laughing with delight. Caitlin's hand clasped firmly in his, Trey started down the aisle, stopping every few feet to be congratulated.

"You're all invited to the reception downstairs in the hospitality center," the minister called.

Trey still held Caitlin's hand, refusing to release her when they reached the hallway. He ducked into a small room littered with guests' winter coats and bridesmaids' pre-wedding clutter.

"Trey," she whispered. "What are we doing? I'm not going anywhere. You can let go of me now."

"No," he whispered. "If I do, your aunts and cousins will take you away."

"Even if they do, I won't go far."

"If you're two steps away, that's too far."

Caitlin's laughing protest faded. His fingers threaded between hers bound them together, and his blue eyes held a fierce possessiveness. But it was the naked vulnerability beneath the fierceness that caught at her heart. She'd wanted him to let her into his heart. Now that he had, they shared an equal power to hurt each other, a concept Trey clearly understood. And feared. She leaned into him, resting her weight against the strength of his, her lips brushing his ear. "I'm never going away. I promise."

He tilted his head to look at her. The tenseness slowly eased from his body as his gaze searched hers. "Thank God," he whispered. "I promise, too." His palm found the slight curve of her tummy beneath the white satin. "I promise both of you. Forever."

Caitlin's eyes misted, her fingers covering his. "Forever."

His mouth covered hers, sealing their private vows. When he lifted his head, they were both breathless, Caitlin wrapped tightly in his arms, her face against the warm curve of his throat.

"Honey?"

"Yes." Her voice was dreamy, disoriented.

"After the baby gets here and we're used to being

parents, how do you feel about having Analisa come to live with us?"

"I'd love to adopt her." Caitlin smiled, her eyes still closed as he pressed her closer. "Our baby will have an instant big sister—just like me and J.J."

Trey closed his hand over her nape, urging her face to his. "I love you, Caitlin Drummond."

And Caitlin had no doubt that the man who hadn't known what love was truly meant the words.

* * * * *